THE ADVENTURES
OF
MARMADUKE PURR CAT

by

CELIA LUCAS

Illustrated by

Susan Cutting

TABB HOUSE

First Published in 1990
Tabb House Ltd, 7 Church Street, Padstow, Cornwall

Paperback   ISBN 0 907018 73 4
Hardback   ISBN 0 907018 87 4

The Author acknowledges the help
of the Welsh Arts Council in writing this book.

Typeset by St George Typesetting, Wilson Way,
Pool, Redruth, Cornwall
Printed in Great Britain by The Guernsey Press,
Channel Islands

For my Mother

and

In memory of Walter Payne,

a friend and gifted artist,
whose portraits of Marmaduke
first inspired this story.

Contents

Chapter One

MARMADUKE GETS A JOB

"THE Catspots of Britain," said Mr Augustus Charabanc, surveying Marmaduke Purr Cat over the top of his spectacles. "Yes, Mr Cat, that's just the sort of holiday programme we want. Something really unusual. The job's yours. Start as soon as you can."

As Marmaduke left the office of Unusual Travel Ltd and made his way across London to Euston Station, his mind raced back over the events of the past few weeks.

It had all started when his friend and master, Mr Roberts, was made redundant.

Someone had to see that Mrs Roberts and the three children - Ceri who was eleven, David who was nine and eighteen-month-old Daniel - were looked after, and if Mr Roberts had lost his job and couldn't get another one it was up to him, Marmaduke Purr Cat, to take over the role of mouse - or, in this case, bread-winner.

It would mean revealing his secret, and after that things would never be quite the same again, but no sacrifice was too great to help the family who had looked after him from kittenhood.

Marmaduke's big secret was, that unlike most cats, he could talk, read and write. He could also impart his gifts to other cats and even other species, just by being with them. What was more, when he was with them, humans could understand other animals as well as himself.

The family had suspected for some time that he

could read, as he was so often to be found with a
white forepaw holding down the page of a book or
newspaper, and when the children did their homework
Marmaduke nearly always jumped up on the desk or
table to see what was going on. But once he had
admitted his talents in so many words, as opposed to
purrs, the cat, so to speak, would be well and truly
out of the bag. Would he ever, he wondered, be able
to return to the uncomplicated world of the cat? It was
a big decision, and what lay ahead frightened him so
much that it made the fur on his spine stand on end.
To calm himself, he turned and gave his coat a quick
lick. As always, the action reassured him. He then set
about making his plan.

First he must find a job. Not as a humble vermin
exterminator; that wouldn't pay enough. A rep. for
pet foods, perhaps? Well, he wouldn't mind sampling
the product but how would he get about the country?
His legs weren't long enough to drive a car or van.

Advertising was a possibility. He was a handsome

animal with a thick ginger coat in shades that ranged from dark marmalade to pale honey. He had a snow-white waistcoat and white paws. Just touching his nose, the tip of which was pink, and spreading over his left cheek was another patch of white fur in the shape of a four-leafed clover. That, everyone told him, was lucky. His great lime-green eyes and long, curling white whiskers were family features of which he was justly proud.

His family were the famous Purrs of Pontybodkin (a little village in North Wales). They are renowned throughout the cat world for the quality of their purr, their big, expressive eyes and the curl of their whiskers.

Marmaduke had emigrated to England to live with the Roberts family in the beautiful city of Chester, just over the border, when he was a six-week-old kitten but it was always his ambition to return one day to the Land of his Fathers, *yr hen wlad fy nghaddau*. That, by the way, is the Welsh national anthem; a lovely tune that Marmaduke would often purr to himself.

The Roberts, too, came from North Wales, from Ynys Môn, the Isle of Anglesey. In ancient days before the birth of Jesus Christ, traders called it The Blessed Isle. For the Romans it was the western frontier of their great empire.

Mr Roberts, too, hoped that one day he and his family would return.

'Advertising', Marmaduke thought. Pretty stupid, really. Who would buy an expensive carpet just so that a cat could get his claws into it or a toilet roll because a dog thought it was a toy? But that was where the money was. Everybody said so. He decided to consult his friend Daphne, the elegant Seal Point Siamese who lived just round the corner. She, he knew, sometimes worked as a photographer's model.

"Wouldn't touch it with a claw if I were you," Daphne told him, with a slight drawl in her miaow. She was a very trendy cat, having lived for several years in Sloane Square in London where the Sloane Rangers come from. "All summer they made me model woollies. Then they transferred me to pet products, and after stuffing me silly with plates of cat food all winter, complained in the spring that I was too fat and gave me the sack. No heart, these advertising agents."

Marmaduke was already a little on the stout side and as he was not a member of ACAT, the Advertising Cats' Union, he might have difficulty in being accepted. He would have to think of something else.

"What are the chances," he asked Daphne, "of getting parts in films or TV? I'm really quite a handsome animal, although I say it myself." And he raised his chin, the better to show the curl of his whiskers.

"Well," said Daphne, looking him up and down with a somewhat scornful gaze, "ginger, you must admit, *is* rather common. After all, there are *millions* of ginger cats around all looking *much* the same. Difficult, really, to tell one from another . . ."

"It's not difficult at all," protested Marmaduke, the fur on his back bristling. "Every animal is different. You've just got to look at the markings on their fur and at their eyes and the curl of their whiskers. Ridiculous."

"Well, I suppose *you* can tell each other apart or life would be very confusing. But to us pedigree cats, you all look alike."

"Pedigree! Fleas! Who wants to come from Siam anyway? Imported rubbish!"

"Mrrrow," growled Daphne, tail lashing.

"And it's not even called Siam any more. It's

4

Thailand. So you're a Thailandese cat, which sounds even sillier."

By now the two cats were sitting about four feet apart on their haunches, staring at each other with blazing eyes and hissing and yowling in an unpleasant manner.

"My mistress says that my pedigree makes me a most valuable animal, acceptable at all the best cat shows," said Daphne haughtily. "But you, you're just an ordinary old tom cat."

"Ordinary old tom cat!" spluttered Marmaduke, jumping to his feet, his hackles up. "Ordinary old tom cat! The Purrs of Pontybodkin, I'll have you know, are famous throughout the cat world. We marched with the Roman Legions, their best mousers. The quality of our purr, the curl of our white whiskers . . ." He was getting extremely heated. His ears lay flat on his head and his teeth were bared.

"Oh sorry, Marmaduke, I didn't mean *you*, of course," said Daphne, realising she had gone too far. She hadn't got many friends, as you can imagine, and she didn't want to lose this one. Besides, if Marmaduke *was* thinking of going into the filming world, he might just make a few contacts that would be useful to her. She was not just a pretty face, oh purr, no.

"Marmaduke!" She was purring softly now. "Marmaduke, I'm seeing my agent tomorrow. Perhaps he can suggest something. After all, yours is a particularly *attractive* ginger, I can see that now. A *real* ginger ginger, a *ginger* of gingers, a . . ."

"Oh, all right, there's no need to go on about it," said Marmaduke. "You've made your point. I'm sure I'll find something. It's just a question of looking, really. So long, Daphne.'' And with a flick of his handsome tail he was off.

He was pawing his way through the Situations Vacant column in the newspaper when he saw it.

'Applicats,' the advertisement read, 'for the post of COURIER with our UNUSUAL TRAVEL SERVICE. No previous experience required but successful candidates will be expected to offer something UNIQUE. Ability to plan own route ESSENTIAL. ECCENTRICITY an asset. Salary EXCELLENT for those with ORIGINAL IDEAS. Applications, please, to Mr Augustus Charabanc, Managing Director, Unusual Travel Ltd, South Kensington, London.'

'Applicats,' said Marmaduke to himself as he ran for his writing paper and pen. 'Applicats. Well, I suppose it's a misprint and they meant *applicants* but it would suit me down to the tip of my ginger tail. I'd do a tour of the Catspots of Britain with all their Catistory and Catlore. Surely *that* would be unusual enough?'

Almost before you could say Kippers he had written his letter of application. For better or worse, he had taken the plunge into the human world. The deed was done, the die was cast. In the last few days he had been in a state of agitation, wondering if he was doing the right thing. Now he felt a weight off his mind. He paw-marked his letter, addressed the envelope and gave a great sigh of relief. His plan was on the way. After giving his coat a quick lick, which made him feel better still, he hurried off with his letter to the local Catmail centre.

The Catmail, as you may know, is administered by bureaucats but the actual carrying of messages - most cats can't actually write - is done by mongrel dogs, known in the trade as underdogs. The service is not quite as fast as the human post but at least messages entrusted to it seldom go astray, so reliable and loyal are the underdogs.

Marmaduke's letter took a week to travel the 200 miles from Chester to the headquarters of Unusual Travel. When he read it Mr Charabanc was delighted. When he saw, to his great surprise, that Marmaduke was a *real* cat and he heard his plan for a tour of the Catspots of Britain he was even more delighted.

"But this is magnificent!" he exclaimed, a wide smile spreading over his plump face. "Highly eccentric! Just the right touch of oddity we need to get this venture off the ground."

He was particularly pleased to have Marmaduke's services, he said, as he had appointed as his other courier, a human in this case, the distinguished Professor Warblemuch, the famous birdsong expert.

"Your two holidays complement each other exactly," he said happily. "But I suppose," he added quickly, seeing Marmaduke lick his lips in a rather sinister fashion at the mention of birds, "I suppose you had better keep out of each other's way, for most of the time at any rate." Then he changed the subject briskly. "The main thing is to give the holiday a real cat flavour . . ."

"Mouse-in-the-hole with sparrow's foot jelly for the first meal, perhaps?" suggested Marmaduke.

"Well, there's no need to go *quite* that far," replied Mr Charabanc with a shudder. "We *are* expecting our clients to be human, remember."

Mr Charabanc then told Marmaduke that he would have their Number Two coach which would be driven by Joe, a great cat admirer. Together they could decorate it in whatever way they thought suitable. His first week's wages, and here Mr Charabanc mentioned a very large sum indeed, would be sent to his Chester address.

"Well so long, Mr Cat. There's a lot of hard work and planning ahead of us. Goodbye and good luck!"

WHEN Marmaduke got home that night, pawsore and weary, his first thought was to tell the family all about his plan.

After supper when he was sitting purring on Ceri's knee, he launched into his story. He moved in such a natural way from Miaowpurrese, which is cat language, to human speech that the family were not quite as amazed by the phenomenon as you might imagine.

"Well, Marmaduke, it's very good of you to do this for us," said Mr Roberts. "I know how much you love home. I am afraid it will be a big sacrifice for you to leave. I really do appreciate it."

"Don't forget us," said Ceri. "People say that cats get attached to places and not people."

"That's just silly," said Marmaduke, lashing his tail in anger. "Some rubbish dreamt up by a dog-loving psychiatrist. Of course I won't forget you. *Dydw i ddim yn anghofio chi*," he added in Welsh. "*Erioed*. Ever."

Coming from North Wales he was, of course, a bilingual cat, or trilingual if you count Miaowpurrese. His family, like many of their countrymen, also spoke both Welsh and English.

"And you will write?" said David anxiously.

"Of course," answered Marmaduke with a purr. 'I'll send you a postcard from every Catspot we visit."

"Oh good. Then I'll be the only boy in school to have postcards from a cat."

"*Bydda yn ofalus*. Be careful and look after yourself," said Mrs Roberts, who knew she was going to miss her faithful companion dreadfully. "And don't forget, *paid anghofio*, to have a saucer of milk a day. It makes your whiskers curl."

"I will," said Marmaduke. "And now, if you don't mind, I'll take a bit of a catnap. My whiskers are drooping with exhaustion. *Nos da*. Good night."

THERE was so much arranging and planning to do that the next few weeks sped by for Marmaduke.

Then the big day came and the family saw him off on the train to London. This time he had an impressive-looking document case strapped round his shoulder. It contained his ticket and a small tin of pilchards in tomato sauce, his favourite meal.

"Good luck, Marmaduke! *Pob lwc*! Goodbye! Ta-ra!" they called as the inter-city train drew out of the station. And poor Ceri felt a big lump in her throat and could hardly keep back her tears.

"He'll be all right, you'll see," her father comforted her. "He's certainly the most capable cat I've ever known."

TWENTY-FIVE people in all had opted for the Catspots Tour. First to arrive at the coach were the Copplestones: George Copplestone, his wife Linda and their nine-year-old daughter Jenny.

Mr Copplestone was tall and serious. His greying fair hair was swept back from his forehead and he wore expensive, tinted spectacles. Round his neck was slung a camera. He looked ill at ease in the casual clothes, open-necked shirt and light trousers, that his wife had bought him for the holiday. Marmaduke sensed he would be much happier in a dark suit and tie, chairing an office meeting or attending a business lunch. Holidays were definitely not his favourite time. He sensed, too, that Mr Copplestone did not like cats.

He was right. George Copplestone, Marketing Executive, (Special Responsibility United States,) did not care for any animals. Farm animals could be tolerated. They, after all, were part of the food industry. But domestic animals he regarded as totally useless, a drain on resources that were better banked or put into stocks and shares.

He knew that Jenny dearly wanted a cat of her own (she obviously took after her mother), and being a generous and loving father, he did not like to deny her. He was just wondering whether to give in when his wife saw the Catspots holiday advertised in a glossy magazine. She and Jenny said they thought it was a great idea and, to their amazement, Mr Copplestone agreed. Privately he saw the holiday as a generous gesture on his part that would release him from any future obligation to purchase a pet. 'Two weeks of Catspots is better than a lifetime with a stupid moggie running up vet bills and eating expensive cat food,' he had said to himself, and besides he was so hard working that he needed a break. As soon as this holiday was over he would be off on one of his many business trips to the United States. His passage to New York on the liner QE2 was already booked and on this occasion Linda and Jenny were to travel with him so that they could visit an aunt in New Jersey. It was a busy life and that was the way he liked it.

Linda Copplestone and Jenny were very much alike with dark, curly hair and big blue eyes. They were both soft-hearted and anxious to please but where Linda was outgoing, at ease in any company, her daughter was shy and lacked confidence. Over the past couple of years Jenny had missed a lot of school through ill health (though she was better now) and this, as well as being an only child, meant she had few friends. That was partly why she longed so much for a kitten. She was thrilled when she met Marmaduke and realised the tour was to be conducted by a *real* cat (you couldn't always believe the advertisements). She was excited - and a little apprehensive too - when she saw more children arriving, hoping that perhaps she would make friends.

"I'm delighted to see you," said Marmaduke, extending a white paw to each in turn. "You're the first, so you've got the pick of the seats. I hope you like the way we've decorated the coach."

"Very nice, Mr Cat," said Mr Copplestone. From a business point of view he was already impressed by the holiday though, personally, he could have done without a cat courier. "Most colourful."

Marmaduke and Driver Joe had been to great pains to decorate the coach with suitable motifs and had painted on it pictures, in very bright colours, of all the famous cats in history from Puss in Boots to Tom of 'Tom and Jerry'.

"Good morning, Mr Cat. I'm Bill MacDonald and this is my brother, Angus. We're supposed to be meeting up with our cousins, the Friendlys."

" Oh yes," said Marmaduke, "Bill and Angus from Aberdeen, Scotland. Your cousins have not arrived yet, but hop in and make yourselves comfortable."

Bill was thirteen years old and Angus twelve. They were both tall for their ages and very fair. Bill's hair was thick with a tendency to flop over his face. Angus's, rather more reddish, was swept back. Bill intended to keep a record of the holiday and had included in his rucksack a smartly bound journal and several ball point pens. Angus was keen on sport and the sea and wanted to be a ship's doctor - with his own ship's cat, of course. Their parents had left them at the coach while they went on to holiday in France.

Next came two young men, also carrying rucksacks. The taller of the two had fair curly hair and freckles and introduced himself as Dan.

"And I'm Ben," said the other young man, who wore his dark hair parted at the side.

"You must be the two student veterinary surgeons from Canada," said Marmaduke, extending a paw.

"Yes, Quebec," said Ben, shaking the paw warmly. "Nice to meet you, Mr Cat."

"Right; in you go," Marmaduke told them.

He felt a bony finger poke his shoulder.

"Mr Cat, if I am not mistaken." The soft, ingratiating voice with the South London twang made Marmaduke wince. Turning, he was confronted by a strange looking man, with one missing front tooth, piercing eyes that were not quite aligned, high cheek bones and a pinched nose. Strands of his darkish hair were plastered down against his skull to hide encroaching baldness and he wore a dingy brown jacket.

"Archibald - call me Arch - Sqynt, at your service," he said. "S-Q-*Y*-N-T."

"I'm pleased to meet you, Mr Sqynt," said Marmaduke with a welcoming purr, but he felt dismayed that he was joining the party. So far he'd liked all his clients, even Mr Copplestone who he knew didn't like cats, but there was something about Mr Sqynt that made him uneasy.

"Call me Arch, Catto. Arch by name and arch by nature, eh? Good one that. Haw, haw, haw! Bit of a wag, bit of a rogue, saucy, clever, some say sly, but no offence meant, eh? See what I mean? Haw, haw, haw!" And he dug Marmaduke in the ribs.

"Yes, very good, er, Arch," said Marmaduke; he didn't take kindly to familiarities. As for the vulgarity of Catto, miaows failed him. Old fashioned in his

12

ways, he much preferred to say Mr, Mrs, Miss or whatever was the right form of address, until he knew people better, or at least until a decent interval had elapsed.

"Is is Catto, or shall I call thee Cat?"

"My name's Marmaduke," said Marmaduke rather tersely. "Marmaduke Purr Cat. Perhaps you'd take your seat, Arch, along with the others?"

Archibald Sqynt described himself as an Information Officer but was, in fact, a business spy. He worked 'in the field', as they say in espionage circles, for a company called BSI (Business Spies Incorporated, Snoopers to the Gentry). In truth they would snoop for anyone if the money was right but director Mr K.G.B. Smith thought the description sounded good. "Respectable, like," he said. His co-director Mr F.B.I. Jones had wanted to add 'By Appointment' and the royal coat of arms but K.G.B. told him you couldn't do that without royal patronage and as yet their clients had not included royalty.

Sqynt's task on this occasion was to snoop on Marmaduke's Catspots holiday on behalf of a rival firm, Jolly Hols, which had been losing business. He had been kitted out with a number of 'listening aids' and been told by K.G.B. to report in by phone to the office three times a day.

"Bugs of every kind in that briefcase, Sqynt, but we likes to call them surveillance devices, eh? Genteel, like," K.G.B. had said. "No harm in being one step ahead, eh, Sqynt?" And Archibald Sqynt had agreed.

It wasn't much of a job but it had its interesting side, eavesdropping on people's private conversations, upsetting business deals before they had even got off the ground. But all his life Sqynt's big ambition had been to find a get-rich-quick scheme so he wouldn't have to work for anybody. He had had many ideas, most of them dishonest, but they had all failed. Meanwhile, to his constant annoyance, he was stuck with K.G.B. and the rest.

No one at BSI had believed the Catspots tour could really have a talking cat. "I want you to find out what kind of hoax this is," K.G.B. told Sqynt. "Get all the evidence you can - pictures, tapes, the lot. By fair means or foul, the usual thing. Get it? Jolly Hols will pay us good money for all the dirt, so do your stuff."

Accordingly, Sqynt had booked his seat, packed his bag with toothbrush and two changes of underpants, taken his brown jacket out of its plastic wrapping and turned up as an ordinary holidaymaker to join Marmaduke's tour.

SQYNT, too, had not expected to find a real cat.

But Marmaduke looked genuine all right. He had given him a good dig in the ribs to make sure of *that*. No false fur or counterfeit whiskers *there*. Sqynt was so excited by the discovery that the sweat stood out on his brow. He wiped it with the sleeve of his brown jacket. A real live talking cat! His head was spinning. There was surely something big to be made out of this!

"May I take your briefcase, Mr Sq . . . I mean Arch?" inquired Marmaduke politely. Mr Sqynt had been so preocuppied with his thoughts, that in wiping his brow with the arm that ended in the hand that held the briefcase, he had got the case stuck in the door.

"No, no Purrface; hand baggage this, got all me personals, like. Purr-sonals, get it, purr-sonals? Haw, haw, haw. Good one that, eh? Haw, haw, haw." And before Marmaduke could get out of the way he had dug him in the ribs again.

'I hope I'm not going to have to see much of *him*,' Marmaduke thought to himself, 'but I suppose this is what *real* work is, taking the rough with the smooth.

Oh dear!' Momentarily he wished himself back at home, a real cat, purring on Ceri's knee, with nothing to worry about but a few wayward mice.

People were arriving fast now: families, students, groups of friends, people by themselves, people of all ages and nationalities. Obviously Catspots had wide appeal.

"Only the Friendlys to come now," said Marmaduke as he totted up. "I wonder where they can be?"

Hurrying up the street, carrying an enormous suitcase in one hand and a couple of fishing rods in the other, came a sandy-haired man in his early thirties, followed by a boy and a girl, each with a battered suitcase and an assortment of plastic bags. About ten yards behind a pretty young woman with long, dark hair clutched a wide-brimmed sun hat to her head with one hand while the other grasped the handle of a large wickerwork picnic basket. She never went anywhere without a well-stocked basket, not wishing that anyone should go hungry.

"I'm Dick Friendly," said the sandy-haired man. "And this is Robert, he's eleven, and Rebecca . . ."

"I'm eight, nearly nine."

"And this is my wife, Rhiannon."

"Pleased to meet you, Mr Cat," said Mrs Friendly, shaking his paw.

"*Sut 'dych chi?*" replied Marmaduke in Welsh, asking her how she was, for he had detected the Welsh accent. "*O ble 'dych chi'n dod?*"

"Where do I come from?" repeated Mrs Friendly. "From Ruthin, in Glyndŵr Country."

"A beautiful spot," purred Marmaduke, "and not far from my own birthplace of Pontybodkin."

He noticed that Rebecca was like her father with thick reddish hair, not dissimilar to his own handsome ginger fur, whereas Robert was dark like his mother. All the family had the most beautiful green eyes.

'Almost as good as cats' eyes,' thought Marmaduke, but he didn't say anything.

Bill and Angus, their cousins, were waving from inside. "Come on," they called. "We knew you'd be late so we saved you seats. Come on."

Mr Sqynt had settled himself in a seat behind Mr Copplestone and Jenny. 'Useful looking chap, that,' he said to himself. 'Must get to know him better. Pity he's brought his family with him.'

"Shall we be on our way then, guv'ner?" called Joe from the driver's seat. He was anxious to get going so he could stop for his first cup of tea with scones, cream and strawberry jam. He was a Cream Tea fanatic and hoped there would be many such teas on this holiday, cats being famous, as he knew, for their love of cream.

"Right, all aboard!" said Marmaduke. "Cases and plastic bags stowed away, Mr Friendly? Right. Catspots of Britain, here we come!"

Chapter Two

ALI KITTEN AND SINUOUS SINGH

THE first Catspot Marmaduke had chosen was the model village at Bekonscot - or Bekonscat, as some prefer to call it - near Beaconsfield in Buckinghamshire.

"Although we can't claim that cats actually built this village with their own paws," he told his party as they got off the coach, "it was built with kittens in mind. It's just the right size for them and they love it."

They children loved it too.

"Look at this little church," called Rebecca. "There's music coming from it, and singing. Christmas carols!" Curious about everything, she was nearly always first to find out what was going on. "Oh Mummy, do come and listen."

Mrs Friendly and the other children went over. Sure enough, the strains of 'Away in a Manger' were coming from the village church. Rebecca, who loved singing, joined in.

"I suppose it must be a tape recorder," said Robert practically. At eleven, you knew about such devices.

"Or a musical mouse," suggested Jenny in a quiet voice and then blushed with embarrassment in case they thought her suggestion stupid.

"Well it *could* be," said Angus, not thinking her stupid at all. "There's an organ playing but there's something else as well. A sort of squeak. Listen!"

They strained their ears and the sound came again.

"It sounds like a call for help," said Bill. "A sort of distress signal." Even as he spoke he was wondering how best to write up the incident in his journal.

"You're right, Bill, it *is* a call for help," said Marmaduke. "Find one of the wardens, quick!"

Mrs Friendly thought he must be out of his furry mind but since there was a uniformed attendant only a few feet away she called him over.

"There's a kitten trapped in that church," Marmaduke told him. "You must get it out."

"Kitten? Nonsense, Mr Cat. That's 'The First Noel' you're hearing. If you wait till three o'clock you can listen to the wedding service, Wedding March and all."

"No thank you, I didn't really want to stay that long. But could you just check that church?" begged Marmaduke.

"More than me job's worth to do that, Mr Cat. I'm not maintenance, see, just patrol."

Marmaduke wondered whether to report him to the TV show that awards jobsworth hats. Another faint mew made him realise that instant action was needed.

"I quite understand," said Marmaduke, "but this *is* patrol work. I have reason to believe there is an intruder in that church."

"Well, if you insist, but it's not *usual*, you know."

Marmaduke could never understand why human beings were always so reluctant to do things that were 'not usual' but he said nothing and watched patiently as the warden climbed down carefully into the village street and took the roof clean off the church.

There, cowering by the organ, was a tiny tabby kitten with a big, black M mark on its forehead.

"Well, bless me if you're not right, Mr Cat," said the warden, handing the tiny, frightened bundle to Marmaduke who took it gently in his mouth by the scruff of its neck.

"Ali, Ali, Ali - miaooooooow - Ali, Ali, Ali!" The strange call came from a distraught mother cat. She ran, limping, along the path to where Marmaduke and his party were standing, her fur dishevelled, her paws dirty, her eyes wild.

"It's all right, Mrs Cat," called Marmaduke; "we've found him."

"Oh thank goodness. I thought when I couldn't find him he'd been . . ."

"Mew, mew," squeaked Ali.

"You bad kitten! You know how worried we Commune cats are at the moment. We've had search parties out all over the forest looking for you. You bad kitten!" And she biffed him smartly on the cheek with her paw.

It turned out that Ali (whose full name was Mahomet Ali, partly because he liked boxing and partly because of the dark M mark on his forehead) had gone missing the night before, when Mrs Cat had taken her seven kittens to the village for the first big outing of their lives. (All tabbies, by the way, have an M mark on their foreheads, It was put there by the prophet Mahomet when he was stroking a tabby one day - or so the legend says.)

Hearing the music in the church and seeing the door open, Ali Kitten had run in to investigate. But T'woo, the village night owl, was watching. Quickly he flew down and shut and bolted the door, thinking to himself that Ali might take a tasty midnight snack later on. Luckily, when it came to midnightsies, T'woo could not unfasten the door, and in the church Ali had to stay. By the time Marmaduke and the children found him he had listened to ten carol concerts, eight weddings, nine Easter services and a couple of funerals, the latter recently included on the advice of a social worker to impart Realism.

"Infants and juveniles," she had said in her 1,000-page report to the Council, "should not be shielded from the more unpleasant aspects of human experience." And everybody at the meeting was so bored they voted for funerals in the model village just to keep her quiet.

"Shall I sing you a carol?" mewed Ali. "I know them off by heart." He was feeling much better now.

"Indeed you shan't, you disobedient kitten," said his mother. She turned to Marmaduke. "Oh what a relief to find him. I know we Commune cats believe in doing our own thing but it's different with your own kittens and I've been worried sick wondering what might have happened to him if . . ."

Before Marmaduke could ask if what, she went on, "You've been great rescuing him, really great. Why not come and have tea with us in the forest? Turn left at the tree that looks like a bulldog, straight on for about one hundred paw lengths, take the right fork past Lion Rock and our home, the Cat's Cradle, is in the next dell. My name's Tiddles, by the way. See you!"

And she ran off, carrying Ali Kitten in her mouth.

"Bit odd, all that carry on, wasn't it?" Mr Sqynt had suddenly appeared at Marmaduke's side. "All planned, was it, just to add a bit of drama to the first day, eh, eh?" And he nudged Marmaduke so fiercely in his already sore ribs he almost fell into the lake they were passing.

"Certainly not," said Marmaduke with indignation. "To think I'd put any animal in a frightening situation like that just for *fun*. Mr Sqynt, how could you!"

"Arch, call me Arch. Arch by name and arch . . ."

"Yes, yes," said Marmaduke impatiently, "but I'd be grateful if in future, Mr Sq - Arch, if you'd refrain from such insulting insinuations."

"My, oh my, we *do* use big words. Rude hints, you mean? No, Catto, not my style. No offence meant,

20

see what I mean? Just wondered. Just interested, see, in how you plans 'n 'oliday. No offence. Haw, haw, haw. . . ."

And if Marmaduke hadn't moved swiftly the bony elbow would have been pounding his rib cage again.

Later, as they walked past a telephone box, they saw Mr Sqynt, notebook in hand, in earnest conversation. When he saw Marmaduke he put down the phone hurriedly, grabbed his briefcase and came out.

"Funny," he said. "Wrong number."

THE forest where Mrs Cat and Ali lived was the famous Burnham Beeches, which stretches for 600 acres over the Chiltern Hills and is part of the ancient forest that covered a much larger area in prehistoric times.

"Anyone who wants to visit Mrs Cat, follow me!" called Marmaduke. He was glad when Mr Sqynt said he had 'other business' to attend to.

It was a glorious day and the sunlight, finding its way through the leaves of the giant beeches, made curious dappled patterns on the ground. The children were enchanted. There must have been hundreds, perhaps thousands, of people in the forest on such a lovely day but they hardly met another soul.

Following Tiddles' instructions, it wasn't long before they reached the Cat's Cradle.

Of the one hundred or so animals that lived there, some were wild and some had escaped from what they called 'irksome domesticity'. Their aim, they said, was 'to get back to nature'.

But the majority were the victims of slum clearance, cats whose homes in the big cities had been pulled down in order to build high-rise flats. Their unhappy owners had to leave their pets while they were rehoused in concrete towers, quite unsuitable for, and indeed forbidden to, animals. If it had not been for the farsightedness of Fabian, the tortoiseshell freedom fighter who searched the country to find a place where he could start a Cats' Commune, most of these faithful animals would have died of neglect, starvation or broken hearts.

"They've fought the good fight," Fabian told Marmaduke. "And now to be faced with this menace - it just doesn't seem fair."

Marmaduke was about to inquire what the menace might be when he was interrupted by Tiddles.

"Come and have a look round," she said, indicating with a paw the dens the cats had made in the hollows of the great beeches. "It's real cosy there in among the fur and dry leaves, especially if there's a crowd of you."

Marmaduke didn't care for crowds. He was a cat who preferred to walk alone. But he purred a polite "Very nice".

"And we have caterwauling session most nights," continued Tiddles. "Like to join us?"

"Some other time, perhaps," murmured Marmaduke. As Tiddles might have said, it was not his scene. "Now what about this tea you kindly mentioned? Is there any chance of some nice scones and cream? Our driver Joe is so fond of cream teas."

"Cream's off," said Tiddles, who had worked in a café.

"Strawberry jam then?"

"Jam's off."

"Then I wonder what you have got for us?

"Let's go see," said Tiddles. She liked to be a cool cat though sometimes her conventional suburban back ground let her down. "Come on."

Marmaduke's party followed Tiddles across the dell to a spot where some trees had been felled. The stumps would make good seats. "Here you are," she said, indicating the ground. "Help yourselves! They're fresh in this morning."

"Oh how dreadful!" exclaimed Mrs Copplestone involuntarily. Before her, laid out neatly, was a row of dead field-mice. They had been caught by the cats of the Hunter Brigade, who were now lined up behind their spoils, purring proudly.

"Shush," said Jenny to her mother, not wishing to hurt the cats' feelings, "they'll *hear* you."

"I feel sick," said Rebecca.

"Look, Tiddles, do you mind terribly if we stick to our own tea?" asked Mrs Friendly. "I've brought the picnic basket with a flask and some cakes. I've even got a scone and cream for Joe. Then there'll be all the more mice for you and your friends."

"Do your own thing, go ahead, that's what you're here for," said Tiddles, waving a paw. "Don't mind us."

And they didn't. While the humans ate the picnic the cats demolished the mice, looking, Jenny thought with surprise, as if they had not had a square meal for weeks. If that was so, it had been very generous of them to offer all their catch to strangers.

It was just at this moment that someone noticed that Rebecca had disappeared.

"It's all right, I'll find her," Marmaduke reassured her parents, sniffing the air.

He sat for a moment longer, with his ears pricked and his whiskers twitching, looking intently in one direction. Then he said "Don't worry." But he *was* worried. His telepathic whiskers told him that there was something very strange and very nasty near at paw, and that Rebecca was in great danger. Curiosity killed the cat, he knew, and like a cat, Rebecca was incurably curious. He must find her quickly.

"Carry on with your tea," he told the others, and

23

then ran off between the trees. He stopped, still as a statue, raised his head and moved it from side to side, sniffing and scenting the air. The smell of danger was stronger now. He started off again, moving more slowly and carefully, his paws making no sound on the forest floor.

He spotted Rebecca by a clump of bracken. She was gazing at what seemed to be an extraordinarily tall thick stick that was swaying in the breeze. Marmaduke could see her head, with its thick red hair in a pony tail, moving in rhythm with the stick, almost as though she were in a hypnotic trance. As he got nearer he realised, to his horror, it was not a stick at all, but a great big snake.

All his senses were now at full alert. With ears pointed forward and body low on the ground for quick action, he moved, rather serpent-like himself, towards Rebecca.

"Hhhhhh," he hissed, baring his teeth. "Hhhhhh."

The snake turned towards Marmaduke. Coiling itself down to cat height, it started swaying in front of him. Its great mouth opened and its forked tongue flickered in and out.

"Ssss-thought you'd ssss-save her, ssss-did you, ssss-smarty puss-ssss," hissed the serpent. "I ssss-shall kill you ssss-both."

Marmaduke stood his ground, trying not to look at the mesmeric eyes. Rebecca had fainted but he dared not run to her side.

"Ssss-surprised to ssss-see me, I ssss-suppose, ssss-smarty puss-ssss?" continued the snake, really enjoying himself. He must have been at least four metres long. "Escaped from a ssss-circus, you ssss-see, and no-one ssss-knows what's ssss-happened to me. All ssss-think I'm dead, the ssss-silly ssss-sausages. But you can't out-sss-smart SSSS-Sinuous

24

SSSS-Singh, the SSSS-Slimiest SSSS-Snake in the SSSS-Circus.''

Just then Rebecca, who had come round from her fainting fit, screamed. Angrily Sinuous Singh turned towards her and prepare to strike. He wasn't poisonous but he didn't suppose she knew that and frightening her might make her faint again. Then, when she was quite helpless, he would coil round her, crush the life out of her and eat her for his supper. He was hungry, and a little girl was just what he fancied.

In that instant Marmaduke leapt in the air, caught Singh by the back of his neck and sank his teeth into the tough skin. The rest of the snake's body writhed and lashed. He was so powerful Marmaduke thought he would have to let go but he knew he must break Singh's neck first or, sure as kippers are smoked, he would swallow Rebecca and maybe himself as well. He realised that Sinuous must be a python, and he

remembered the story that he had been told of the python who had eaten a fourteen-year-old Malay boy in Indonesia. He was not going to let this one eat Rebecca. With all his cat's concentration he clung to Sinuous Singh, keeping himself anchored to the violently heaving snake, while he bit again and again into the thick neck.

At the tea party, the humans had been wondering uneasily what had happened to Rebecca and Marmaduke, but had not wanted to upset their hosts by going in pursuit, even though the cats themselves were miaowing agitatedly amongst themselves. Rebecca's distant screams galvanised everyone, cat and human, into action. They all jumped to their feet, and a moment later a crowd of cats, followed by puffing and panting humans, poured into the clearing by the bracken clump. They could hardly believe their eyes when they were met by the sight of Marmaduke and Sinuous Singh, locked in mortal combat. A stream of cats rushed to help Marmaduke, but now Marmaduke's sharp teeth had finally broken the neck bone and Sinuous Singh was in his death throes. For a few more moments the snake continued to writhe, but at last the powerful tail was still, and only then did Marmaduke dare let go.

He staggered back, utterly exhausted, his fur bedraggled, his beautiful whiskers and the lucky white four-leafed clover mark on his face stained with black blood.

Then a tremendous caterwauling broke out.

"The monster's dead! . . . Marmaduke's slain the monster!"

"Miaow, miaow, we're saved!"

"Rejoice, cats and kittens, rejoice greatly!" cried Fabian the freedom fighter, (who was given to flamboyant speech). "Bring forth the hero, that we may honour him with glad miaows and a chorus of joyous purrs! For he has delivered us from the terror that slithered by night and devoured our kittens and stole from us our rightful prey, the mice of the fields. So that we have hungered and died for lack of food and known not what to do. Bring forth the hero, I say!''

It was just as well he used those words, thought Marmaduke to himself, however odd they might sound, coming from a cat. Because *someone* was going to have to bring him forth. Certainly he would never manage it on his own four paws.

Then he felt a soothing wet cloth on his face and heard a boy's voice saying ''Come on now, Marmaduke. That's it, easy.'' He opened his eyes and saw Angus bending over him. ''Better?'' he asked.

''Yes, better,'' said Marmaduke. ''What's Fabian on about?''

''He wants to show you to the crowd. You're a hero! You've killed the monster that was eating all their kittens *and* their mouse supply too. Shall I carry you?''

''Oh, purr I wish you would.''

''*Mor ddewr a llew*!'' It was Mrs Friendly's voice.

'As brave as a lion,' thought Marmaduke. 'As weak as a kitten, more like. *Mor wan a blewyn.*'

There was a buzz of voices, miaows and purrs all about him. Even the air was full of noise; the grateful chirps and tweets of the birds of the forest. For Sinuous Singh had not only enjoyed eating kittens and mice, he had also been fond of a nice bird's egg, particularly for breakfast.

''See the conquering hero comes! Sound the trumpets, beat the drums!'' miaowed Fabian loudly.

27

He realised they had no trumpets or even drums but he had once lived with an actor and thought the couplet appropriate.

As Angus carried Marmaduke forward, a great sound like the whirring of a million vacuum-cleaners filled the forest. It was the Chorus of Purrs, every cat and kitten purring its heart out, an accolade only bestowed on the few.

When the purring died down Fabian told Marmaduke, still in Angus's arms, about the Reign of Terror they had been living through.

"Almost every night kittens went missing and at first we just didn't know what had happened to them. Then one of our hunters, out mousing, spotted this monster. We'd seen grass snakes and adders before, of course, but nothing like this."

"So *that's* why Tiddles was so worried about Ali Kitten," said Robert, who had joined the group now he knew his sister was all right.

"And *that's* why the cats were so pleased when we left them those mice for tea," said Jenny. "I *thought* they looked half starved!"

"Nasty things, pythons, " said her father. "I saw quite a few when I was in Malaysia. They have been known to grow to eight metres in length. This one was quite big. You did well, Marmaduke. Congratulations!"

Congratulations? What was he, George Copplestone, Marketing Executive (Special Responsibility United States), doing congratulating a cat? It was all very strange. But he could not help being impressed by Marmaduke. What intelligence, what versatility, what courage! Perhaps he had been wrong about cats. Certainly this one was not stupid.

"We ought to report the incident to the police," he continued, taking charge of the situation. "I don't mind taking the head if the rest of the party will help with the body."

"Right," said Marmaduke. "If you could organise that, Mr Copplestone, I'd be most grateful. I don't think I . . ."

"No, of course not. You take it easy. You've done more than your share for one day."

Rebecca and her parents couldn't thank Marmaduke enough.

"You're the best animal in the world," said Rebecca, burying her nose in his fur and giving him a great big kiss.

"*Diolch yn fawr iawn. Wyt ti'n gath garedig. Wir,*" said Mrs Friendly, stroking his matted fur.

"Yes, thanks a million," echoed her husband. "You really are a good cat. Rebecca's curiosity is always getting her into trouble. Thank goodness you knew what to do! You saved her life - you're a brave animal!"

"*Cath ddewr iawn.* A very brave cat," said Mrs Friendly.

Bill and Angus decided to take turns carrying Marmaduke back to where the coach was parked and most of the adults volunteered to help with the corpse of Sinuous Singh. Luckily the police station was not far from the car park. The officer on duty was rather surprised at having to take a python into custody but he was glad that at least it was a dead one.

When he had taken Marmaduke's statement, he explained "It's definitely the one from the circus. Escaped in transit when the van was involved in an accident on the motorway. Goodness knows how it made its way here without being spotted. It went missing over a year ago and there were search parties out for weeks, looking for it. They even called in a Home Office mongoose. Then we had that severe winter and all the experts said if it was still alive the

frost and snow would certainly finish it off, it being
from India and all that. So we stopped worrying. We
took down the 'WANTED' notice with the 'mug shot'
and closed the file.

"If it hadn't been for your prompt action, Mr Cat,
we could have had a very nasty situation indeed on
our hands. Thank you for your co-operation. You
will, of course, receive the reward of £100."

"Oh, purr, thank you!" said Marmaduke, and he
thought of his family at home and how pleased they
would be. "Purr, oh purr."

Back in the coach, Mr Copplestone told Mr Sqynt
all about the events of the day.

"Remarkable animal," said Sqynt. "Bit of a prize
fighter, then? Bit of a wrestler? Pity we can't do
something with him, what with your connections in
the United States, eh, eh?"

"What do you mean?"

"Use him in a line of business like, eh, eh?" And
he dug Mr Copplestone in the ribs.

"Do you mind?" said Mr Copplestone.

Chapter Three

SAMPSON, THE BIONIC CAT

THEY were on their way to Oxford when Marmaduke taught them the Purr Cat song.

"It's my family song," he explained. "I'll sing it through and you join in the chorus. I expect you'll recognise it. It goes to the tune of the Welsh folk song 'The Ash Grove'."

He drew in a big breath and started:

"Oh, we are the Purr Cats,
The Purr Cats of Pontybodkin,
Oh, we are the animals
mWith melodious purr.

"We've got ginger fur and
    snow-white waistcoats
And long, white curling whiskers,
Lime-green eyes, pink noses
And thick bushy tails.

"Oh, we are the Purr Cats . . .
    etc.

"Our coats are like marmalade,
Our socks are like snowflakes,
Our eyes are like saucers
That gleam in the dark.

"Oh, we are the Purr Cats . . .
    etc.

"We speak both Welsh and English
And also Miaowpurrese,
We read and we write
And we do simple sums.

"Oh, we are the Purr Cats . . .
    etc.

"We're rather on the stout side
But that's no disadvantage
Our mousing and our ratting
Are second to none.

"Oh, we are the Purr Cats . .
    etc.''

In true conductor's style, Marmaduke brought the song to an end.

"Here we are!" he said, as they rounded a roundabout and drove over a bridge with a tree-lined river below. "The high street, or the High as it is called here. The University has lots of colleges and it started in the thirteenth century. Some of the buildings date back to that time." He believed a courier should be informative.

"But what's it got to do with cats?" asked Jenny. She was getting a lot bolder now and making friends. Marmaduke was glad. Of all the children, this shy little girl with the lovely deep blue eyes was, perhaps, his favourite.

"Without cats, this University would probably not exist," he told them, with no trace of doubt in his voice. "In those days, the Middle Ages, this place was full of scholarly cats, the mouse population being even larger than it is today. And in 1346 the Convocation of Ratters and Mousers met here to try and devise a plan to deal with the notorious Black Rat, whose fleas carried the Plague germ.

"Two thirds of the population of this country were wiped out by the Black Death, as it was called, but things would have been much, much worse had it not been for those brave ratters who risked infection themselves to save their human friends."

"Surely cats didn't get the Plague, did they?" asked Angus, stopping Marmaduke in full flood. He was interested in plagues.

"Well, no, they didn't," admitted Marmaduke with a cross "brrrp". He was an animal who did not care for interruptions. "But rat bites are extremely dangerous and can produce blood poisoning and all sorts of things like that, so what I said about those brave ratters is perfectly true. They *did* risk their lives. Tragically, their only reward was to be cruelly persecuted." He gave a low growl.

"What do you mean, Marmaduke?" asked Bill. He wanted to get his facts right for his journal.

"It was that silly witchcraft business. For several centuries people became obsessed about witches. They said they were to blame for everything: crops that failed, milk that turned sour, people who went mad or were struck down with mysterious illnesses. Thousands of people, most of them kind old women with cats, were denounced as witches and burned at the stake. And many of their cats, accused of being in the service of the devil, perished with them."

"Oh, how dreadful!" chorused the children.

All except Bill, that is, who asked: "Well, *were* they witches and *were* the cats the devil's servants?"

"Of course not," said Marmaduke crossly. "It's just that human nature, unlike animal nature, always looks for someone or something to blame when things go wrong.

33

"Not that witches don't exist," he went on with a quick, suspicious look over his shoulder, which he speedily disguised as a lick to his fur. "I think they *do*, but there aren't all that many around."

"No, 'cos they all went up in smoke!" joked Angus, and everybody laughed.

Marmaduke, on the other hand, was distinctly ruffled. Twitching his tail in angry flicks of annoyance and fixing Angus with a piercing, lime-green gaze, he said icily, "I had an ancestor who was burned at the stake. He was ginger, with the longest whiskers in recorded history. A most unpleasant way to go."

"Oh, Marmaduke," said Jenny, feeling ashamed that she had laughed at Angus's joke, "if I'd been there I would have rescued him."

And Marmaduke knew she meant it, although he could not know how far she would go one day in his defence.

"Indeed, it is no laughing matter," continued Marmaduke sternly. They had left the coach by now and were walking round the town.

"Look, here's the Martyrs' Memorial marking the spot where three bishops were burned at the stake."

"*Bishops*? Were *they* witches?" asked Rebecca, wide-eyed, wondering how that could be.

"No," said Marmaduke. "Their names were Latimer and Ridley, and later Archbishop Cranmer, and they were burned in 1555 on the orders of Queen Mary, Bloody Mary, because she was a Catholic and they were Protestant. A terrible thing to do in the name of religion. No animal would behave like that. And the other side were no better." He growled.

"But Latimer's last words were famous," he continued. "Bravely, as the flames crackled round him, he cried out: 'Be of good comfort, Master Ridley. Play the man. We shall this day light such a candle, by

34

God's grace, in England as I trust shall never be put out.' "

Bill liked that quotation. He was scribbling hard.

"Bit silly, isn't it," he said, "burning each other when we all worship the same God?"

"Humans!" growled Marmaduke. He wasn't going to be brought into *that* controversy.

Instead he suggested that those who wished should buy their postcards now and he would arrange to send them, pawmarked and free of charge, by Catmail.

"Catmail? What's that?" asked Robert.

"It's a postal service for cats. It's run by bureaucats who employ mongrels, known as underdogs, as runners. There's a centre here in Oxford. It's very efficient. No message sent by Catmail has ever been lost. I use it all the time."

The conversation reminded him of his promise to David at home in Chester to send a postcard from every Catspot. His terrible adventure with Sinuous Singh had put postcard writing right out of his mind. He must send one now. Apart from anything else, he wanted to tell the family to expect him and his party in Chester in a few days' time. While he was about it, he would send a message to Daphne, his Siamese friend, as well. She was a bit snooty and affected but he liked her and it would be nice if she could join them.

"You tell a good story, Marmie old cat, but where do you get your info., like?" The voice was that of Mr Archibald Sqynt.

"From books, of course," said Marmaduke, rather shortly.

"What? Books from libraries, like? Old books?" pursued the irritating Mr Sqynt.

"Sometimes. It varies," said Marmaduke. His tail began twitching. He was getting angry.

"Make notes then? Got them with you, have you?

35

Give us a bit of a peep, bit of a squint. Squint? Sqynt. Get it, get it? Haw, haw, haw.''

Marmaduke backed away swiftly from the bony elbow.

"No, I *haven't* got anything you can see," he replied, fur bristling. "I don't make notes, I have no need to. I am a cat blessed with a remarkable memory. It's one of the attributes of the Purrs of Pontybokin, Mr Sqynt."

"Arch, call me Arch. Arch by name and . . .''

"Oh, all right, Arch," he said crossly. Then, turning to the others, he called "Come on now, everyone, we're off to meet some friends of mine."

As Marmaduke's party followed him back up the High, Mr Sqynt joined Mr Copplestone.

"Remarkable animal that, eh, eh?''

"He is indeed," agreed Mr Copplestone. And then added, to his own great surprise, "I'm beginning to enjoy this holiday.''

A pity, that, thought Mr Sqynt. Perhaps he could get his mind back on business?

"Do a lot of work in the States, then, Special Responsibility and all that?'' pursued Mr Sqynt.

"Yes; as it happens I'll be going over on a business trip immediately after this holiday." And briefly Mr Copplestone outlined his work schedule and told Mr Sqynt of his plans to travel to America on the QE2. Not many people were interested in his job. He was flattered that Mr Sqynt was.

"A cat like Marmaduke would go down a bomb there, eh? Talking cat and all that. Reading, writing, singing pop songs even? Eh, eh?'' And he dug Mr Copplestone in the ribs. Which was a mistake.

"Do you mind?'' he said crossly. "You nearly had me in the street.''

They had reached a college with a tall, stately tower. One by one, through a small archway, they entered the college and there, standing on the lawn in front of some ancient buildings, was the imposing human figure of Magnus Longclaw, Regius Professor of Catistory. He wore robes of scarlet and navy-blue silk, and on his head was a special academic hat, a square mortar board with a tassle.

"Professor Longclaw, I'm delighted to meet you," said Marmaduke, extending a paw. "I've read some of your books and found them most interesting; most."

"Nice of you to say so, Mr Cat. Most people here never praise anything. No generosity of spirit, the academic world, I'm afraid. Oh well, *tempus fugit*, so we must get on with our tour."

"I beg your pardon," said Marmaduke, not understanding the foreign phrase.

"Time flies," explained the professor. "Latin. We use it quite a bit here."

He showed them round his college, which was called Magdalen and pronounced Maudlin.

"It was built at the end of the fifteenth century," he told them, "and every May Day morning at sunrise the choir sings from the top of the tall tower. All the birds of the air join in."

Marmaduke licked his lips.

"What a delicious – er, I mean delightful – prospect."

"Your slip of the tongue did not escape me, Mr Cat," said Professor Longclaw, who was the human world expert on cats and their deeds, good and wicked, throughout history. "But I gather from my illustrious colleague Professor Warblemuch, whom you are to meet later in your holiday, that a 'Paws Off' pact has been made."

"Yes, purr, it has," said Marmaduke. "It goes against the instincts a bit, I confess, but I gave my word to Mr Charabanc and a cat's word is his bond."

37

Then Marmaduke suggested that his party might like to relax with a picnic tea on the river (he had already bought scones, cream and strawberry jam as well as cakes, jellies and biscuits).

"My friend Sampson, the Bionic Cat, has offered to punt us," he said. "I'm not big enough to manage one of those long poles myself, but he can."

"The Bionic Cat; who's he?" asked Rebecca.

"Wait and see," was all Marmaduke would say.

When they reached the river the answer to Rebecca's question became obvious. There, standing on his hind legs and leaning nonchalantly against a punt pole, was a handsome black and white cat almost two metres in height.

All five children: Jenny, Rebecca, Robert, Bill and Angus, piled into one punt with Marmaduke. The Bionic Cat stood at the back, grasping a punt pole in his powerful claws.

He was magnificent. He manoeuvred the shallow vessel with the greatest skill out from the little jetty and soon they were gliding smoothly up river, leaving the grown-ups in their punts far behind.

The trees grew thickly on either side, often arching right over the water to meet in the middle.

"How ridiculous! A cat with a punt pole!"

The mocking voice came from a brash-looking young man who was punting downstream towards them. His girl friend, to whom he was obviously showing off, giggled and agreed.

"He's out of all proportion. Eaten too many mice, have you, fatty?"

As they laughed and jeered at poor Sampson, the top of the young man's pole got caught in the branch of a tree, and in a second, the punt had shot forward leaving him clinging awkwardly to the pole. Gradually, he slithered down until he was up to his neck in

chilly water. Now his girl friend was laughing at *him* instead.

"Serve him right," said Marmaduke, "for insulting Sampson like that!"

Robert Friendly was just wondering himself how Sampson came to be so big when Marmaduke interrupted his thoughts.

"I expect you'd like to know about Sampson, and as he doesn't mind, I'll tell you. He is so big because of an experiment they did in the laboratories here."

"Oh, how *awful*," said Jenny. She was very soft-hearted.

"Well, yes, it isn't very nice. Some poor cats do get used for experiments but we won't go into that now. Anyway, Sampson was given hormones and he simply grew and grew."

"It didn't happen to any of the other animals," Sampson explained from the end of the punt, "and they still don't know why it happened to me. Some mistake mixing their chemicals. Anyway, I'm *unique*!" And he preened his great, rope-like white whiskers with his free paw. "One scientist said I should be exhibited in a zoo but fortunately I have Friends in High Places – " Sampson swelled with importance – "and *that* idea was soon quashed. There were Questions in the House, I believe . . ."

"What house?" whispered Rebecca.

"He means the House of Commons. Parliament," explained Angus.

"Oh."

"If you're a bionic cat, what else can you do?" asked Robert. He was a practical boy and wanted to know.

"Just you watch," said Sampson. With that, he gave the punt a massive push with his back paws, and using the pole as a lever, he vaulted high into the air.

40

The punt took off at about forty miles per hour. It was like shooting the rapids. And as they hurtled along, clinging to the side of the craft, screaming with excitement and delight, they saw Sampson sailing through the air above the tree tops. As the river broadened out the punt slowed down and Sampson began to descend, punt pole still in paw, until, soft as a ball of fur, he alighted in his same place.

"I wish *I* could do that," said Robert.

"Well, you can if you like," replied Sampson. "Come on."

And without more ado he scooped Robert, who was quite a big boy, under his arm, and with an even more massive push, the two of them shot up into the sky.

This time they sailed right over the city, Sampson using his bionic tail as a rudder to steer him in the direction he wanted to go.

After that, of course, all the children had to have a go.

"Bless my soul," said Marjorie Jackdaw to her neighbour Pauline Pigeon that evening at roosting time. "What *is* the world coming to? Not all that many years ago the skies were ours, give or take a bee or two. Then came those horrible, noisy aeroplanes and those beastly, luminous flying saucers that everyone makes such a fuss about. Now, as if *that* wasn't enough to frighten the feathers off your poll, we get airborne cats and flying children."

"Yes, indeed," cooed Pauline Pigeon in agreement. "I think we should make representations to the Air Corridors Board. If this sort of thing is allowed to continue there'll be nowhere to stretch a wing in peace."

"Feline Flying, No! Feathers Rule, OK!" squawked Marjorie Jackdaw, who prided herself on her ability to compose slogans.

And as the bells chimed out all over the city of dreaming spires that evening, every bird from sparrow to starling, blackbird to barn owl, joined in a noisy chorus.

"Feline Flying, No! Feathers Rule, OK!"

AS soon as possible Mr Sqynt hurried to the telephone to report the incident to his office. He was put through quickly to K.G.B. but he could tell his boss didn't believe a word he said.

"You sure you're not losing your marbles, Sqynt?" said K.G.B. "Got any pictures to prove all this?"

Arch had to admit that he hadn't. "Mislaid me camera, see. Well, left it behind in the coach in a manner of speaking."

"You forgot it, you mean, you incompetent fool. That's not what we pay you good money for. Our client, Jolly Hols, needs evidence so they can move in and take over Unusual Travel's ideas. Do them down right and proper. Then we're on a percentage, see? They're not interested in a load of old fairy tales."

"But everything I've told you is true," protested Sqynt. "You know me, K.G.B., honest Arch, never knowingly told a fib . . ."

"Look here, Sqynt," said K.G.B. "You've been on this case a few days now and all you've come up with is rubbish. You say Marmaduke is a real cat, a talking cat. That's good, that's fine. But why no tape of his voice, eh?"

"I recorded it all, honest I did boss, but when I comes to play it back – nothing. Perhaps there's something wrong with the batteries, duds like."

"Duds? I know who's the dud all right," stormed K.G.B. "And there's another thing. Yesterday you gives me some cock and bull story about a cat killing a snake and then you tells me you weren't even there to

42

see it. And no pictures neither. It ain't good enough, Sqynt."

"I thought I'd attend to other business like . . . " began Mr Sqynt tamely.

"Your business, Sqynt, is to be on the spot. Get it? Or *I'll* put you in a spot all right. Out on your dirty, scruffy neck. Is that understood?"

"Yes, sir," said Mr Sqynt and put down the phone. As he came out of the box, wiping his sweating brow on the sleeve of his brown jacket, he saw the children on the other side of the road.

"Any luck," called Bill, "with your phone call?"

"No," said Mr Sqynt with a scowl. "Wrong number."

Chapter Four

THE WITCH OF WOOKEY

ARCHIBALD Sqynt was fed up. Fed up with having to ring his office three times a day. Fed up with BSI (Snoopers to the Gentry). What right had K.G.B. to talk to him like that, to accuse him of making things up and threaten him with the sack?

'I'll show them what they can do with their stupid job,' he thought to himself. 'I'll think of a plan so I'll never need their beastly job again as long as I live. I'll . . . '

Of course. The get-rich-quick scheme he had been looking for all his life was here, plain as a pikestaff, in front of his very eyes. Marmaduke. The animal who could make all his dreams come true. If he could get Marmaduke to work for him he could ditch BSI and set up on his own. That would teach them. He could start an entertainment agency, perhaps? 'Sqynt and Son'. That sounded good except he hadn't got a son and didn't much want one. 'Sqynt and Cat' then?

Yes, that was better. But would Marmaduke want to go into partnership with him? He had a feeling he didn't like him much.

His thoughts turned to Mr Copplestone. Now *there* was a man of enterprise. Mr Sqynt had spotted that straight away. *And* he had contacts in the United States where all the money was. If only he could interest *him* in a business proposition. 'Sqynt and Copplestone, Cat (ar) Acts a speciality'. He chuckled to himself. 'That was good, cat(ar)acts. Bit of a wag, our Arch, bit of a caution, eh, eh?'

But Mr Copplestone wasn't co-operative either. He

had tried approaching him on two occasions, once after that snake business and again in Oxford, but he hadn't seemed interested. He was supposed not to like cats but now he said he was enjoying the holiday. Soon he would be as silly about cats as the rest of them. What was he, Archibald Josiah Sqynt, to do? Here was a golden opportunity for making a fortune staring him in the face and he didn't know how to use it. He sighed deeply.

"Are you tired, Arch?" asked Marmaduke considerately. He had noticed Sqynt making telephone calls and felt it was a shame he should have to bother with whatever it was while he was on holiday. Particularly as he always appeared to get the wrong number.

"No, purrface, just thinking," replied Mr Sqynt.

"Well, we're almost at our destination," said Marmaduke.

They had been travelling south west, and now they had arrived.

Wookey Hole, near Cheddar in Somerset, is a great cavern that has been gouged out of the limestone cliffs by the River Axe. The children were excited at the prospect of the visit as they had all heard of the famous Witch. The adults were looking forward to it too.

"Before we go in, let me treat you all to ice-creams or coffee," said George Copplestone.

"Oh, thank you!" "Strawberry for me, please." "I'll have chocolate." "Just vanilla, if you please, purr." The orders came in.

As George and his wife Linda sat together sipping their coffee, he confided "I'm really enjoying this holiday. It gets better every day and it's nice to see Jenny so happy and making friends. Marmaduke has brought her right out of her shell."

Refreshments over, they all made their way up

a little hill to the cave entrance where their guide was waiting. As they followed him down the narrow path into the dark interior, the children couldn't help shivering in spite of their warm anoraks. It was not so much the cold, though it *was* colder inside than out, but the eeriness of it all that made the goose pimples rise on their arms and necks. Strange shadows formed on the cave's walls and ceiling and all the time they could hear the plip, plip, plop of invisible water drops.

Then they saw her, a great dark rock, the Witch of Wookey. Black and menacing, her cloak flecked with silver in the artificial light, she brooded over the cavern as if it were still her domain and the lake beyond, her magic cauldron.

"Is she real?" asked Rebecca in awe.

"Well, she was once," Marmaduke told her. "A witch *did* live here long ago. According to legend, a monk followed her into the cave one day to try and catch her. But it was dark and he lost sight of her, so, as a precaution – just to be on the safe side, you know – he sprinkled holy water all around him. And a few drops just happened to fall on the witch. She let out a terrible scream and then there was silence. Nothing except the drip, drip, drip of water from the cave's ceiling.

"The monk ran out, terrified, but he decided he must find out what had happened. So the next day, this time with his lantern and a fresh supply of holy water, he went back. And there was the witch, turned to stone, a great black stalagmite . . . "

"What's a stalag, stalag . . . ?" asked the younger children.

"Stalagmite," said Angus, who knew about these things. "Well, it's a sort of pillar of lime formed over thousands and thousands of years by water dripping through the rocks, and stalagmites go

46

up and stalactites go down. Isn't that right, Marmaduke?"

"Yes, that's right, Angus," said Marmaduke. "The limestone that makes them, you see, dissolves in the water," he added for the benefit of those who were still looking puzzled.

Robert had another question. "If it takes thousands and thousands of years for a stalag, stalagmite to form," he asked, "how did the witch become such a big one just overnight?" He was a great one for practicalities.

"Well," answered Marmaduke, scratching his head with his forepaw and wishing that children didn't ask so many awkward questions, "well, she was pretty big to start with and was probably thousands and thousands of years old too. But funny things happen, you know, when you're dealing with witches; real witches, I mean." And he shuddered as he felt a chill, like a witch's bony finger, creep down his spine.

"Have you seen her little dog?" asked the guide, who seemed quite happy to share his commentary with Marmaduke. "He's there, at her feet."

"Oh, isn't he sweet!" said Jenny and Rebecca together.

"There's no doubt," continued the guide, "that a witch lived here once. Archaeologists have been doing excavations and they found the skeleton of a woman with a dagger and a witch's crystal ball by her side. Careful now! This way, please! Follow me!"

Mr Sqynt was fascinated by the Witch. As he gazed into her hard, glinting eyes he became more determined than ever to use Marmaduke to make himself rich by fair means or foul. The possibility that others might get hurt in the process did not trouble him in the least.

George Copplestone was staring at the Witch, too. Some strange magnetic force seemed to hold his eyes.

Suddenly he felt very cold and irritable and he was conscious of the length of time he had been in the dank cave and of the desert of wasted time that had passed since breakfast, let alone since the start of this ridiculous holiday. Only a few minutes ago it had seemed fun, but now his feelings had changed radically and it appeared boring and stupid. Why, he wondered, had he agreed to come in the first place? Cats! He had never really like them and as for holidays, they were a complete waste of time and money. He longed to be back at work, busy with some new plan that would perhaps make his fortune. If the truth were known, he was pretty well off already but in that instant as he looked at the Witch he had a desperate longing, a burning desire, to be very, very rich. It was greed such as he had never felt before. It gnawed at his bones and turned over his stomach so that he nearly cried out with the pain.

'How can I be rich?' he asked himself. And the answer came loud and clear: 'Marmaduke! Use him, exploit him, cheat him.' Briefly he thought 'That's no way to think of Marmaduke,' but as quickly he stifled his conscience. He had had a brilliant money-making idea, and that was the important thing. Briskly, with impatience at the silly people round him, who wanted to do nothing but talk to cats and go on boring trips round the country, he turned away to follow the guide round the rest of the caves, anxious to get out of them as soon as possible.

The children were so absorbed by all the different strange and beautiful shapes in the caverns that it wasn't until they came out into the daylight again that they realised Marmaduke was missing.

''Where can he be?'' asked Rebecca. ''Cats hate

the cold so he surely won't want to stay in the caves."

The grown-ups, with driver Joe, of course, had gone on ahead to order cream teas in the café, leaving the children, as they thought, in the capable paws of Marmaduke. Bill had joined them to catch up with his journal.

"Let's call him," said Angus, going back to the cave entrance. "Marmaduke, are you there?" But only his own words answered in mocking echo.

Then Jenny said "Listen! I thought I heard a miaow. There it is again! 'Miaow, please help me,' he's saying."

They all listened hard but could hear nothing – nothing but the cold waters of the Axe lapping against the sides of the cavern and the drip, drip, drip of water through the rocks.

"Are you sure, Jenny?" asked Angus. "Where's the miaow coming from?"

"I *think* it's the Witch."

"The Witch!" said Rebecca. "But he wouldn't stay with *her*, he didn't even *like* her. Didn't you notice him shivering when he saw her?"

"Well, that's it, then," said Robert sensibly. "He's probably still there, too afraid to move. You know what it's like when you're frightened."

"Come on," said Angus, "let's go and find him. Keep your ears pricked for miaows, all of you." And he led the way back into the cave, followed by the other three children. As they went, Rebecca suddenly felt very alarmed but, remembering how Marmaduke had saved her, she steeled herself to carry on.

It seemed to have got several degrees colder than when they were in the cave only a few minutes earlier. Theirs had been the last party to go round that day and there was no one else now in the Great Cavern or

49

Witch's Kitchen. Luckily the floodlighting was still on or it would have been as black as pitch.

"Marmaduke," called Angus. "Are you all right?"

"Marmaduke Purr, are you there?" echoed Jenny.

"Marmaduke, where are you?" called Robert and Rebecca.

The Witch towered above them, the jagged rock of her cloak gleaming cruelly in the artificial light. In her eyes was an evil glint betraying something the children could not quite fathom at first. Then Angus defined it. "It's greed." And he spoke the thought that was in each child's mind. "Yes, it's greed!"

"Stop!" cried Jenny suddenly. "I heard him. I heard another miaow. He's frightened and in pain."

The lights played tricks with their eyes as they scanned the craggy outline of the great stalagmite. One minute they thought they saw a clump of ginger fur, the next it was gone.

Then Rebecca was sure. From under the Witch's arm poked the tip of a ginger tail!

"Right, I'll have to climb up there somehow," said Angus. "He must be stuck."

"How on earth did he get there?" asked Rebecca, puzzled.

"And why on earth did he get there?" asked Rebecca, puzzled.

"And why on earth did he *want* to?" said Robert. "There'd be no mice or birds there. It's silly doing things without a good reason."

"Don't let's worry about that now," said Angus.

"Listen," said Jenny, "another miaow!" She couldn't
think of anything except her friend Marmaduke and wouldn't be happy till he was safe.

Climbing the stalagmite was not easy, and at times Angus thought he would never make it. By the time he reached the spot where the tail was, his hands were cut and bleeding from contact with the sharp stone. Luckily he was so numbed by the cold he could hardly feel the pain.

But when he got there, he found it *was* Marmaduke. Somehow he had got a claw caught round a stony icicle right inside the Witch's shawl and, struggle as he would, he could not shake himself free.

With his feet resting precariously on folds in the Witch's cloak and his left hand gripping her shoulder, Angus tried to ease his right hand into the narrow space beneath the Witch's arm where Marmaduke was trapped.

"I can only just reach his paw," he called to the children below. "He seems to have a claw caught in some sort of trap. Easy now, Marmaduke. We'll get you out, I promise."

But there was more confidence in his voice than in his thoughts. The claw would not budge.

Meanwhile Rebecca, standing below, had an irresistible urge to test the temperature of the lake, the Witch's Cauldron. She wanted to know if, being a cauldron, it was hot. Quietly she stole away from Jenny and her brother and knelt down to put the tip of her finger in the water. It was cold, but not very cold. She put in her arm, up to her elbow, just to see if she was right. Suddenly from the depths of the still water came an icy current which gripped her arm so that she jolted forwards, almost tipping into the lake. She braced herself against the force that tugged so fiercely at her arm, now submerged up to her shoulder, that she began to feel that she would be pulled beneath the surface. She screamed. Robert and Jenny rushed over, only just in time to save her from being dragged in altogether.

"Won't you ever learn?" said her brother crossly.

"As if we haven't got enough problems with poor Marmaduke!"

"Thank goodness you're all right," said Jenny rather more sympathetically.

"It's no good," called Angus from high up on the stalagmite. "I've got cramp in my arm." He had been fifteen minutes trying to free Marmaduke. "I'm coming down."

"Let me have a go," said Robert.

He climbed up the same way his cousin had done but he was smaller and his arm was just not long enough to reach the end of the trapped paw.

"I can't reach," he called.

By now, Marmaduke was sounding distraught.

"We'd better get the student vets," said Angus. "Marmaduke may need medical treatment and they'll know what to do."

Jenny and Rebecca said they would fetch help while the boys stayed with Marmaduke. Within minutes they were back with Dan and Ben. Bill followed, clutching his journal and a guide book. Soon Dan was shinning up the stalagmite.

"OK, Marmaduke, just relax and we'll have you free in no time," said the student. But as he struggled with the claw he, like Angus, began to lose confidence.

After half an hour of trying everything he could think of, Dan's training told him that something drastic would have to be done if he was to save the shivering and exhausted animal.

"Ben," he called.

"Yes, Dan, here."

"We're going to have to amputate the paw. Can you have the instruments ready? Jenny, Rebecca, will you give him a hand?"

Their professor had told them always to carry an Animal First Aid Kit with them. "You never know,"

he said, "when it may come in handy." And how right he had been.

"OK, Dan," Ben called back. "Everything in order. I'm coming up now."

The children were aghast.

"Isn't there any other way?" asked Jenny. "Poor little animal!"

"Just give it *one* more try, just in case," begged Rebecca, her own nasty experience in the lake quite forgotten.

Marmaduke's miaows were getting weaker and weaker. He was a young, strong cat but Dan was afraid his heart could give out under the strain.

Obviously something terrible had happened to him, something far more serious than just getting a claw caught, though that, in the circumstances, was bad enough.

Dan braced himself to make one last effort. By now he had cramp in both arms and he decided, if he couldn't free the claw this time he would let Ben have a go and if that didn't work they would have no alternative but amputation.

His fingers twisted once more round the now swollen paw and with all the force he could summon he pushed sideways against the trapped claw. "Oh, for the strength of the Bionic Cat!" he exclaimed.

As he said the words he felt a tremendous surge of warmth in his arm and, for an instant, a tenth of a second perhaps, he was as strong as Hercules – or, in this case, Sampson. The claw came free – and the power went as quickly as it had come. He id not mind, for that strength had done its work.

Gripping Marmaduke unceremoniously by the scruff of his neck, Dan dragged him from beneath the Witch's cloak.

"It's OK," he called. "I've got him – Here, Ben, take him," he said, handing the semi-conscious animal carefully down to his fellow student.

"Right, I'll give him a shot of something to get the circulation going," said Ben. "An hour or so longer in there, my friend, and you'd have had it," he added to Marmaduke. "You'd have been mousing in the Happy Hunting Ground in the Skies. There, you'll be OK now."

And from somewhere deep inside, in that purr-box that cats keep a secret of their own, came a faint, low rumble of furry thanks.

Rebecca took off her warm blue cardigan and wrapped the exhausted animal in it while Jenny massaged the damaged paw and stroked his cold fur. The white four-leafed clover mark on his face, she noticed, looked brighter than ever. 'It must be lucky for him,' she thought.

By the time they got him outside, where Mrs Friendly was waiting with a thermos of warm milk and a saucer, Marmaduke was almost himself again.

In a breathless mixture of human speech and Miaowpurrese he told them what he could remember of his ordeal. "Just after I'd told you about the Witch I got a funny shiver down my spine," he said, shivering again at the memory.

"I *told* you he was shivering," said Rebecca.

"Then," continued Marmaduke, "a tremendously strong mousing scent came upon me. I've never known anything quite like it. It was as if all the mice in Naples – and there are plenty there, you may be sure – had made their nests just a paw's length or so from the tip of my whiskers.

"I just *had* to investigate; I couldn't stop myself. After that, all I remember is climbing and climbing and the scent getting stronger and stronger. I had to go on. I suppose it was like being hypnotised. And all the time I could hear someone calling, 'Marmaduke, Marmaduke, come to me, come to me, and I will feed you on fresh pilchards and cream for ever!' I didn't even remember to ask whether the pilchards would have tomato sauce with them, I was so carried away . . . "

"Oh, Marmaduke, you're making it up. *Wyt ti'n dweud celwydd*," said Mrs Friendly. "You couldn't possibly have heard that. *Amhosibl*. There was no sound at all in the cave except the echo of our voices and the lapping of the water."

"Go on, Marmaduke," said Ben, the student. "This could be very useful for my thesis."

55

"Well, there's not much more to add," said Marmaduke, examining the strained claw of his right forepaw. "I saw something run past in front of me, put out a paw to snatch it as any cat would, and the next thing I knew something had snapped down on my claws and I was trapped."

"Oh Marmaduke, how awful," chorussed the children.

"Yes, it was. And as it gripped me I heard the most horrible cackling like the sound of shattering ice and the more I struggled the louder it grew till I thought my head would burst.

"It was only then that I realised where I was – trapped under the Witch's cloak. Until then I'd been in a sort of dream."

"Under a spell, you mean, Marmaduke," said Jenny. "Oh, how horrible. The wicked, wicked Witch!"

"That's great, that's fantastic!" exclaimed Bill.

"What do you mean?" said Marmaduke, aggrieved. "I was very nearly an ex-cat."

"No, I don't mean your *experience*. That was terrible, of *course*. But this guide book explains it all. It says that 'Wookey' comes from the old English word 'wocig' meaning a trap for animals! So that's why you got trapped in the witch's cloak."

"And *that's* what happened to the little dog," said Robert. "He was trapped and then turned into a stalac, no, stalag-mite."

"Poor little thing!" said Rebecca. " – I wonder how many more animals she's trapped in that way?"

"Paw a bit easier now, is it, Marmaduke?" asked Angus. He was wondering whether he should be a vet instead of a doctor.

"Yes, thanks. And a million purrs for finding me

56

and trying so hard to free me. You saved my life. Yes, thanks to all of you. Multiple, multiple purrs.''

"How can you have multiple purrs?" mused Jenny, trying to imagine how they would sound. Something like the chorus of purrs at the Cats' Cradle in the forest, most likely.

Her speculation was interrupted by her father, who had scarcely said a word since leaving the cave. It was almost as though the Witch had cast a spell on him, too.

"You're wasting your time here fooling around with these stupid trips," he now told Marmaduke. "I do a lot of business in the United States; that's the place to be, that's where the money is, not in this dump of a place. You could make a fortune telling your stories on lecture tours in the States. I'd be your manager.''

"But I don't want to leave this country," said Marmaduke. "It's the best in the world and, besides, my family lives here. I'd never leave it, never.''

'There goes a brilliant idea,' thought Mr Copplestone crossly, 'unless I can get him to change his mind. That's the trouble with cats, basically stupid. Here's a golden opportunity to make a fortune staring me in the face and I don't know how to use it.'

His thoughts were quite remarkably like those of Mr Sqynt.

WHILE the others went to look round the gift shop, Mr Copplestone bought himself a cup of tea and sat down at a corner table to contemplate.

"Penny for them," said Mr Sqynt.

"Penny for what?" asked Mr Copplestone. "I've had enough tea. Don't like the stuff much anyway.''

"For your thoughts, of course; your inmost, secret thoughts. Thinking about that cat as a business proposition, were you? Bit of a money spinner, bit of an earner, eh, eh?'' He put his own cup of tea down on the table and took a seat next to Mr Copplestone.

"How did you know?"

"Blessed with intuition is Arch. Cunning, see, Arch by name and . . . "

"Yes, yes," said Mr Copplestone impatiently. He felt extremely irritable, as one often does when sickening for a cold. "Well, what do you think?"

"Think you're right, dead right. Good idea, lecture tour. Brilliant. Good thinking. One snag."

"Oh?"

"Marmaduke won't co-operate. You heard just now. He's not prepared to set paw out of this country. And he won't change his mind either. He's a stubborn bundle of ginger fur, our Marmie."

"What do you suggest?"

"What don't *co-operate* gets *co-erced*, don't it? Eh, eh?'' He edged nearer Mr Copplestone.

"What do you mean?"

"Capture him, of course. Catch him. Cat in the bag. Force him to work for us."

"Us?"

"Yes, you and me. Partners. Make a fortune, eh, eh?'' And edging nearer still, he dug Mr Copplestone in the ribs.

"Do you mind?" said Mr Copplestone irritably.

"Sorry, no offence, no harm meant, just a gesture like, way of expressing myself. Fancy another cup of tea?''

"No, I can't stand the stuff. Let's get back to business. If we take him against his will he's not going to want to give lectures and then we would be stuck with a disagreeable animal on our hands."

Mr Sqynt had thought of that. "Yes, that's why we must do something else. Sell him outright to some big

58

organisation or other for a lot of dough, like, and leave *them* with the problem.''

"But what sort of organisation?" Mr Copplestone wracked his brains to think of any useful contacts he had made as Marketing Executive (Special Responsibility United States). Zoos wouldn't want him. *Their* animals didn't talk.

"What about Hollywood?" suggested Mr Sqynt. "I suppose he's quite a good-looking animal as far as cats go." He slurped his tea and wiped the sleeve of his dingy brown jacket across his mouth.

'Disgusting habit,' thought Mr Copplestone; but business was business and this was the sort of talk he liked. It was almost as good as being at the office. "Look, Arch," he said, "let me give this some thought and get back to you."

"Daddy!" It was Jenny.

"What do you mean by interrupting me? Go away, I'm sick of the sight of you!"

"George!" called his wife, "come and look at this!"

"Can't you see I'm busy? Just leave me alone, will you?"

He turned back to Mr Sqynt. "Bloody pests those two. Where were we? Yes, cat in the bag. Can you see to that?"

"No problem. Leave it to Arch, Arch by name and arch . . . ''

"Yes, yes," said Mr Copplestone irritably. "Well, get going as soon as possible. At least it will put an end to this boring holiday. I take it we are partners in this?"

"Partners," said Mr Sqynt, extending a bony hand. He couldn't believe his luck. What a welcome change had come over George Copplestone! He could almost believe the Witch had something to do with it.

"Operation Marmaduke," said Mr Copplestone.

"Operation Marmaduke," said Mr Sqynt, and they shook hands.

Chapter Five

WHITTINGTON FAIR

MARMADUKE was shaken by his experience with the Witch of Wookey. His paw still ached in spite of the prolonged licking he had given it - a sure cure for pretty well anything - and he hoped that the next day would be as pleasant and uncomplicated as he had planned. He had arranged it long ago when he first got the job, as a 'fun day' for his party. It wouldn't be restful exactly but it should provide him with light relief and take his mind off Wookey. Surely nothing could go wrong in the company of so many of his own kind?

"You've all heard of Dick Whittington,"he said, as they sped northwards from Cheddar. "Well, today we are going to visit the place where he lived and meet the descendants of his famous cat."

"I hope there's something to do there besides shaking a lot of paws," whispered Bill to Angus.

"Yes, there is," said Marmaduke, whose ears were sharper than human ones. "Every year the Whittington cats hold the famous Whittington Fair and today is the day of the fair. The village, by the way, is Newent, near Gloucester."

The exclamations of delight about the fair had scarcely died down when they arrived at the village green. Waiting to greet them were cats of every colour, shape and size: black cats, brown cats, grey cats, tawny cats. One extremely large white cat called Polar appeared to be in charge.

"Go and enjoy yourselves," he said. "Everything's free; you are our special guests."

"Thank you," purred Marmaduke.

It was far and away the most unusual fair any of them had ever seen. It was completely run by cats.

'Guess my Weight! Three guesses for one herring's head!' a notice read. Behind it sat an absolutely vast tabby with a white star of fur on his forehead. His name was Hefty Herbert.

"Oh, that poor cat!" said Mrs Friendly, who hated to see an animal in what she thought of as distress. "However did he get to be that fat? Shouldn't he go on a diet? Oh dear!"

"Shush," said Marmaduke, "or he'll hear you. I suppose *you* think its pretty unhealthy but *he's* very proud of being the Fattest Cat in the World."

"In the world!" exclaimed Robert Friendly in wonder. "Can I have a guess? Oh, I've got no herring heads."

They all realised at once that they just hadn't got the right currency for the fair. Polar had said everything was free but how could they explain that to the cats?

"Oh Marmaduke, what *shall* we do?" wailed Rebecca. "We won't be able to go on *anything*."

"Don't worry," Marmaduke reassured her, "Polar has organised tokens. Here they come!"

They turned and saw a scruffy grey cat dragging a sack. "With Polar's compliments," she said. "Have a good day!"

Pawing out the tokens, Marmaduke noticed that two of his party, Mr Copplestone and Mr Sqynt, were missing.

"Where are they?" he asked.

"They said they were going to look for a telephone," said Jenny. "I don't know why."

"Arch is always on the phone," said Angus. "I can't think what he finds to say."

"Well, he doesn't have much luck. Whenever you ask, his reply is always 'Funny, wrong number'," said Bill. And everyone laughed.

Everyone, that is, except Jenny and her mother. They were worried. Ever since Wookey Mr Copplestone had been different. He seemed pre-occupied with his thoughts and had hardly addressed a word to either of them except to say something unpleasant. When Linda had asked him if anything was wrong he had just told her to mind her own business. The only person he seemed to have any time for was Mr Sqynt. Last night he had been out late with him until about two o'clock in the morning and now he was off again.

"Never mind," said Linda to her daughter. "I expect he got a chill in that cave. He'll be all right tomorrow." But she had her doubts. The only thing to do was to try and enjoy the fair with the rest of them. Jenny had so looked forward to this holiday, particularly after her illness, that she mustn't let anything spoil it for her.

"Come on, what shall we do?" she said.

They decided to guess the weight of Hefty Herbert.

"Two stones," said Linda.

"Thirteen kilograms," said Jenny, using the metric scale.

"Wrong," said Hefty, a smile spreading over his fat face, "three stones, thirteen pounds, or twenty-five kilograms, if you prefer it. Almost as much as you, little girl."

Next they all tried their hand, and Marmaduke his paw, at 'Catch the Mouse'. The only one who could catch anything was Marmaduke and he only managed four out of six.

"Great," cried the children. "Fantastic! You clever cat!"

"Well, it's not all that good, really," said Marmaduke, and he was telling the truth, for modesty was not one of his virtues. "At one time I could have caught all six. I'm a bit out of practice."

Then Bill said "Let's try the Ghost Train."

"Roll up, roll up, for a JOURNEY that will make the fur on your neck creep and FRIGHTEN your whiskers RIGID," called the Ghost Train attendant, who was coal-black from tip to tail and had luminous green eyes like flying saucers.

He had no need to advertise. The queue of cats and kittens wanting to be 'scared out of their fur' was longer than a giant rat's tail.

The cats had rigged up the Ghost Train inside an old barn, and as the children and Marmaduke stood waiting they could hear from within the muffled sound of hysterical caterwauling and the excited mews of kittens and young cats.

At last it was their turn. They piled into a six-seater carriage, Marmaduke and Jenny at the front, Rebecca and Robert behind them and, at the back, Bill and Angus. With a loud caterwaul the double doors ahead of them burst open and they shot off into the dark interior. Rats' tails brushed their faces; vampires swooped, bared fangs dripping with blood. They turned quickly and the head of a great hound confronted them, jaws gaping. The carriage jolted back and forth and then plunged into an abyss where ghostly skeletons of cats danced and caterwauled. Up again, round about, pitch darkness. Then a blinding flash and ghosts everywhere, floating in white shrouds, wailing. The children screamed with excitement. Marmaduke's fur stood on end. Suddenly one of the ghosts lunged towards them and grabbed at Marmaduke.

Jenny was so scared by the horrors of the ghost train that she had been clinging to Marmaduke throughout the journey. Now as she felt him being pulled away she clung even harder. Marmaduke himself gave a loud miaow of terror. Instinctively, his free paw went out to defend himself and with claws unsheathed he scratched at the belligerent ghost. He seemed to tear at flesh, which was strange because he thought ghosts were insubstantial things you couldn't get your claws into. With a yell, the ghost let go, stumbled back and fell.

"Bother that cat. Bother that girl!" they thought they heard a human voice whine, but the sound was drowned in caterwauling.

At last they were out in the open again.

"Oh, that was scarey," said Robert. "Can we have another go?"

"I didn't like that awful noise," said Rebecca. "What was it?"

"Caterwauling," answered Marmaduke. "Some of the best. But if you don't want another go I'll come with you to something else. One of those ghosts nearly got me and it's given me quite a turn. Silly really." And he turned round and gave his fur a good lick.

"Funny," said Bill, "I thought I heard Mr Sqynt's voice in among all those ghosts."

"He must have been in another carriage," said Angus.

"I suppose so," said Marmaduke, but he felt uneasy just the same. He was glad Jenny had been holding onto him so tightly. *She* seemed to think the incident was all part of the excitement of the ride. Well, it probably was. He mustn't start imagining things.

And indeed, Jenny decided to join Robert, Bill and Angus for a second turn.

"Come on, Rebecca," said Marmaduke. "What do *you* fancy doing?"

"The fortune teller, please," said Rebecca.

"I don't usually go in for that sort of thing myself," said Marmaduke as they set off hand in paw, "but I suppose if you insist . . ."

As they approached the fortune teller's tent, which was some distance from the Ghost Train, they head a female cat's voice singing:

"Are you going to Whittington Fair?
(Herrings, pilchards, kippers and bream.)
Remember me to a cat who works there.
He is known as a mouser supreme."

"I recognise that song," said Rebecca, who knew a lot about music. "I thought it was '*Strawberry* Fair'."

"Well, perhaps it *is* in human language," said Marmaduke, "but I prefer the feline version."

Catalonian Carmen (for that was the fortune teller's name) was a smallish grey cat with blazing green-yellow eyes. She wore a kerchief round her head and a gypsy's shawl.

"Like your paw read, my dear?" she asked as Marmaduke approached the tent. "I do palms, too, if your friend would like a reading."

"Well, I . . ." Marmaduke wasn't sure if he really wanted his fortune told. After all, what will be, will be, and perhaps it is better not to know.

"She's great. Worth every pilchard," said a large tabby, who was standing nearby. "Got extra-sensory perception in her whiskers, that one."

"What's that?" asked Rebecca.

"Well, all cats' whiskers are sensitive to moods and atmosphere," said Marmaduke, "but hers must be particularly sensitive. Through them she picks up vibrations which tell her what has happened and what may happen in the future. That's the idea, anyway."

He was not altogether convinced, but that didn't bother Rebecca one bit.

"Oh, let's go in. Come on, Marmaduke, do."

Hand in paw, they entered the tent where Catalonian Carmen was sitting ready at the table. She had known straight away, when she first spoke to them, that they would be customers and had gone in to prepare her crystal ball.

Rebecca was first.

"Let me see your palm, me dear; right hand first, then left," said Catalonian Carmen with a quiet purr. "You are like a cat, too curious for your own good. This has got you into serious trouble twice in the very recent past, once in a forest, once by an underground lake. Am I right?"

"Yes," said Rebecca. "How did you know?"

"By the twitching of my whiskers," replied Catalonian Carmen, still purring. She reached for the crystal ball. "Now concentrate, my dear, and I'll see what the crystal reveals."

She lent over the ball, which glittered and twinkled a greenish-gold, seeming to catch the light from her blazing eyes. "You, my dear, will sing for your supper," she purred. "You will sing on a big stage and everyone will cheer and clap and be happy."

"Oh, how exciting," said Rebecca.

Catalonian Carmen turned to Marmaduke and took his paw. "Now let's see what I can tell you, my fine ginger friend."

Slowly her purr changed to a growl. "Danger," she growled, "I see danger. You have an enemy who is plotting against you. Beware the false friend. And I see another who has been led astray. Beware them! Beware the place where the water flows in a man-made river! Beware the mystery in the thorny bush!"

"Oh dear," said Marmaduke.

What a mistake it had been to show his paw, he thought to himself, but he was too polite to say so to Catalonian Carmen. Anyway, he thought again, what was he, a cat of the world, doing believing in this sort of thing? Surely it was a lot of nonsense, hocus-furry-pocus?

"Danger lurks," continued Catalonian Carmen, still growling. "But I see the mark of a four-leafed clover on your face. This lucky sign may save you as it has in the past. Cats have nine lives but those with the four-leafed clover mark have nine times nine."

'Just as well if your predictions are to be believed,' thought Marmaduke, but he said nothing.

"Let me look in the crystal," said Catalonian

Carmen. "It never lies." She drew the ball towards her. Now it looked murky yellow, the colour of storm clouds. "Confinement, darkness, despair," she said. "But wait, the crystal lightens. You can be saved. You must seize the bright umbrella and open it in the blazing sun."

"Umbrella in the blazing sun? What do you mean?" miaowed Marmaduke.

"Enough, I've said enough," said Catalonian Carmen. "Seek no more, my friend, but remember my words." And she got up from the table and turned away.

"What a load of rubbish," said Marmaduke twitching his tail tetchily, as they left the tent and walked over to rejoin the others. "Man-made river! Thorny bush! Umbrella in the blazing sun, indeed!" But he would be glad when he could drown his fears in a saucer of pilchards in tomato sauce. What a strange holiday this was turning out to be!

"I'm going to be a singer, Mummy," cried Rebecca. "Catalonian Carmen said so."

"That's nice," said her mother.

At that minute Polar came strolling over.

"I hope you'll all stay for tea," he said. "We've put on a special feast. Sandwiches, cakes, jellies, scones with cream and strawberry jam and pilchards in tomato sauce. No catspread is complete without pilchards."

"No indeed," purred Marmaduke. "How very kind!"

They were to have tea in the old timbered market hall in the village centre. Mr Sqynt and Mr Copplestone had already made their way there and had started on the sandwiches.

"You made a right mess of that, Arch," said Mr Copplestone, helping himself to another chicken sandwich. "We could have got the whole thing tied up by now and have had done with this ridiculous holiday."

"I did my best," said Mr Sqynt.

"Don't speak with your mouth full," said Mr Copplestone crossly. "Look, you've spat sandwich all over my new trousers."

"Sorry, no offence," said Mr Sqynt, wiping the sleeve of his dingy brown jacket across his mouth. "Ouch," he exclaimed, "Ouch."

"What's the matter now?"

"It's me arm," squealed Mr Sqynt. "That 'orrible cat scratched it when I tried to catch him. Beastly sharp, those claws of his."

"Why weren't you wearing your jacket? I've never seen you with it off."

"I couldn't wear a jacket pretending to be a ghost, could I? Ghosts don't wear jackets."

"Heaven preserve me from idiots!" cried Mr Copplestone. He was beginning to think he had made a bad mistake going into partnership with Sqynt. "It's easy enough, surely, to catch a cat? Why didn't you just grab him and run?"

"It wasn't my fault," said Mr Sqynt crossly. "It was that wretched girl of yours, your daughter. If she hadn't had hold of him I'd have got him. Scrunch!" And he squeezed his fist and twisted his wrist as though wringing poor Marmaduke's neck.

"Yes, she is a pest," agreed Mr Copplestone, who usually would not have a word said against Jenny. "Next time I'll make sure she's nowhere near. Now, how about next time? We mustn't make any more mistakes. There could be big money involved if we get the right buyer."

"Big money, eh?" Mr Sqynt saw visions of riches ahead. And riches brought honours. Sir Archibald

Sqynt. Lord Sqynt of Surbiton. Your Grace, Duke Sqynt (was that right?) He heaved a wistful sigh.

"Are you with me, Arch?" asked Mr Copplestone. Really, this man was most irritating. "What are you going to do about catching Marmaduke? We must get him, and the sooner the better. I can't negotiate good terms without a reasonable prospect of having the merchandise."

The absurdity of thinking of Marmaduke merely as merchandise did not cross his mind.

"Right," said Mr Sqynt, bringing himself back to reality. "Bit of a plot, bit of a plan, bit of a scheme. See this briefcase here?"

"Yes."

"Well, it's full of bugs; surveillance devices we like to call them. Genteel, like." He thought of his employer K.G.B., whom he planned to let down as soon as he possibly could. 'Serve him right, the old tyrant,' he thought. Out loud he continued "I'll bug Marmaduke's room, listen in when he's on the phone to that Charabanc person in London so I can find out exactly where we are going and lay a bit of a trap. Then I'll get my mate Ronald to do the necessary."

"Yes, but warn him to be careful. Damaged goods won't be any use to us."

"Leave it to Arch. Arch by name and . . ."

"Yes, yes, all right," said Mr Copplestone, as much irritated as ever by Sqynt's refrain. "Here are the others. Let's behave normally. We don't want to arouse suspicion."

Jenny came running over to her father.

"Oh, Daddy, we've had such a lovely time. We've been on rides and the Ghost Train and . . ."

"Why tell me? I'm not interested," snapped her father.

71

Chapter Six

SAINT DAPHNE OF CHESTER

JENNY was in tears. "I don't know what's the matter with him," she confided in Rebecca. "He says such terrible things. Last night I heard him telling Mummy he was sick of both of us. He said we were a drain on his expenses, just parasites. Without us, he would be rich, he said."

"I'm sure he didn't mean it," said Rebecca. "Perhaps he's got stomach ache. Or toothache. That can be *awful*. Even *my* dad, and he's pretty good tempered, gets moody when he's got toothache."

"I don't think it's that," said Jenny. "He just seems bored with us and bored with the holiday. He doesn't seem to want to do anything with us any more."

"He wasn't like that at first," said Rebecca. "He came with us to the forest and was awfully good about carrying Sinuous Singh to the police station." She shuddered at the memory. "And at Wookey he was so kind, buying us all ice-creams."

"Yes, that's what he used to be like," said Jenny. "Before Wookey. I know he likes to work hard and cats are not his favourite things but he's always been good to us. Now everything's changed. All he wants to do is talk with that horrible Mr Sqynt. It's almost as if they were plotting something, the way they sit with their heads together."

"Come on you two or I'll have to go without you," called Joe from the driver's seat. "Hurry up!"

Jenny dried her eyes and the two girls ran over to the coach.

"Where have you been?" snapped her father. "Can't you see you've kept everybody waiting?"

Their destination that day was Chester. The plan, Marmaduke told them, was to look round the city, his city, and then meet up with his human family for a cream tea by the river.

"Good thinking, Marmaduke," said Joe. He was putting on weight from all the delicious teas he had been eating.

"It was a Roman city," continued Marmaduke; "the headquarters of the Twentieth Legion, and many of the cats you'll see here today are descended from the noble animals who marched with that legion all the way from Rome."

"Did your ancestors march with the legion, Marmaduke?" asked Rebecca.

"Yes," he said, "the Purrs of Pontybodkin were that great legion's best mousers. We guarded the granary in what is now Watergate Street and slew hundreds and thousands of rats and mice."

"Are you a Cheshire cat then, Marmaduke?" asked Jenny. "Like the one in the book?"

"*Alice in Wonderland,* you mean? An excellent story and a splendid cat but . . . "

Bill interrupted. "Pontybodkin, Marmaduke, where is it?" He was studying his map.

"It's not far from here, in North Wales."

"North Wales, where Mum comes from," supplied Robert.

"Yes," said Marmaduke, "and we'll be going there soon, but now let's enjoy today."

"Did you hear that?" whispered Mr Sqynt to Mr Copplestone. "We'll be going to Wales. Remote and rural. That's when we'll get our chance. I'll give my mate Ronald a bell and put him on alert for the transportation of goods, like."

"And I'll make my arrangements," said Mr Copplestone. Suddenly he knew exactly what to do with Marmaduke. It was that question of Jenny's that had clinched it. He was excited and couldn't wait to get going with his plan.

"We'll go our own way, Arch and myself," he told Marmaduke as they got off the coach. "Business."

"Just as you like, Mr Copplestone," said Marmaduke. "Perhaps you would like to join us later for tea by the river with my family?"

"Yes, we'll do that. Come on, Arch." Mr Copplestone set off at a brisk pace for the city centre, closely followed by an out-of-breath Mr Sqynt.

"What's happening, Georgie?" Mr Sqynt was on first name terms now with his partner. "What's all the rush?"

"I've got it, Arch, I've got it!" said Mr Copplestone. "The Master Plan. It will make us both rich, very rich, riches beyond our imagination. It can't fail. Why didn't I think of it before? I suppose that girl's got some uses after all."

"What girl? What uses?" panted Mr Sqynt.

Mr Copplestone didn't answer. Instead he stopped outside a smart hotel and said "Right, we'll go in here so I can make some trans-Atlantic calls. You wait for me at the bar and order some drinks. Here's a tenner."

After about half an hour he returned.

"Well, what is it? What's the plan?" asked Mr Sqynt anxiously.

"The Cheshire Cat, that's it," said Mr Copplestone. "Jenny mentioned it and then I knew. Cheshire Cat. *Alice in Wonderland. Disneyland.*"

"I don't understand," said Mr Sqynt. "What do you mean?" Had his partner in crime, usually so businesslike, taken leave of his senses, he wondered?

74

"What I mean, Arch my friend, is that I've sold Marmaduke, smiling ginger face and all, to Disneyland in California, as the original Cheshire Cat from *Alice in Wonderland*."

"Disneyland? The place with all those cartoon animals like Mickey Mouse and Donald Duck? What's the Cheshire Cat got to do with that?"

"Walt Disney made the Alice story into a film with that stupid grinning cat as one of the stars. So you see, it's right up Disneyland's street. We won't get the cash till we hand over Marmaduke but they are talking in millions."

"But didn't Marmaduke say he came from Wales?" asked Mr Sqynt. He wasn't usually a stickler for the truth but he was confused.

"North Wales? Cheshire? What's the difference? Nobody knows, nobody cares. Certainly no one in California will be any the wiser."

"No, I suppose not," said Mr Sqynt, who wasn't too sure of the difference himself.

"The main thing is that he talks and grins and they are going to pay us good money for him. So from now on, whatever anybody says, he's the Cheshire Cat."

"Right," said Mr Sqynt.

"And it's about time we signed a formal agreement. Operation Marmaduke. I've drafted two copies. Here."

The signing was done in a matter of seconds and, businesslike as ever, Mr Copplestone continued: "Now it's up to you to catch him. We mustn't delay."

"It's like I said: Wales, remote and rural. I'll do it there."

"And make sure that mate of yours, Ronald, doesn't knock him about. Disneyland is paying for a smiling cat, remember, not a miserable-looking moggie. Do I make myself clear?"

WHILE Mr Copplestone and Mr Sqynt were scheming, the rest of Marmaduke's party were enjoying themselves in the lovely bustling city of Chester, with its unique two-tiered streets known as Rows, its bright shops and historic walls. The walls encircle the city and Marmaduke thought the best way to see everything was from the top of them. As he took his party round, he stopped to indicate places of interest, the cathedral, King Charles's tower, the racecourse. Finally they reached the Pepper Gate, one of the four gates into the city, and looking down, they saw below them the great half circle of a Roman amphitheatre.

"The other half has not been excavated yet," explained Marmaduke, "but there are . . . "

He stopped mid-sentence for he had heard the unmistakable tones of a rather peevish miaow. His ears pricked forward.

"I'd recognise that miaow anywhere," he said. "It's Daphne, my Siamese friend, and she's in trouble!"

The children had heard all about Daphne. They knew she was a famous model, with one of the longest pedigrees in the land, and that for many years she had lived in Sloane Square, a most fashionable part of London. Marmaduke had sent her a message by Catmail from Oxford and they were looking forward to meeting her. They hoped she wouldn't be too grand to shake paws.

Daphne did indeed consider herself a cat above the rest. She preferred not to mix with the local, 'provincial' cats but she made an exception of Marmaduke. "Ginger *is* rather common," she would say to herself, "and *whatever* he says about being a Purr of Pontybodkin, it's not a *patch* on having a pedigree like *mine*, but he *is* entertaining."

In her hour of need, though, Daphne would have accepted help from any animal, whatever the colour of his fur or the length of his pedigree. But no one seemed to be taking any notice. She mewed again; long, loud and rather pettishly.

Marmaduke and the children were not long in locating the source of the complaining mew. Just near the amphitheatre, below the walls, is a Roman Garden with columns and a hypocaust (a water-heating system for baths) and other bits of Roman masonry. And there, sitting on top of a tall pillar in the middle of the garden, was a strikingly beautiful Siamese cat.

"Daphne, what on *earth* are you doing there?" called Marmaduke from his perch on the wall. "And how in the Cat's Whiskers did you *get* there?"

No cat could possibly have climbed the pillar. Or have jumped onto it. Except, perhaps, the Bionic Cat, and Daphne, though beautiful, was not bionic.

"Oh, Marmaduke, thank goodness you've come," mewed Daphne. "Oh darling, good, kind Marmaduke! I've never been so badly treated in my life. I'll complain to my Union, ACAT. It's disgusting! They think just because one is a cat they can use one any old how. And me, a superstar! I'll never forgive them, I'll scratch their eyes out, I'll . . . "

"For goodness sake, Daphne, calm down or you'll fall off that pillar and break a paw," warned Marmaduke, still at a loss to understand how any self-respecting animal could have got in such a ridiculous position in the first place. "Keep still and we'll come and rescue you."

"There's a ladder just over there," said Bill, pointing across the street to where two men were painting the outside of a house. "Let's see if we can borrow it."

77

So Bill, Angus and Marmaduke went in a deputation to the painters while Jenny, Robert and Rebecca made their way into the garden to comfort Daphne.

"It's ever so high," said Robert. "How long have you been there?"

"Ever since dawn," miaowed back Daphne.

"Oh, poor little animal!" said Jenny. "How lucky it's not raining."

"Now *there's* a stupid remark if ever I heard one," said Daphne, tail lashing. "It's *unlucky* being stuck up here in the *first* place, so I can't see how it's so *lucky* it's not raining. If it *were* raining, it would just be even unluckier."

"Oh, I'm sorry, I . . . " began Jenny, but by this time Daphne's attention was elsewhere. The boys, helped by the two painters, were arriving with the ladder. It was very long and exceedingly heavy. Without the men's help they would have had a job carrying it.

"Best let me go up," said one of the men. "We're insured, see, for climbing ladders and we don't want any of you lot going up and breaking your necks, do we?"

So with his mate holding the bottom steady, he climbed up to get the now highly nervous Daphne.

"Come on puss, good puss," he called when he reached the plinth where Daphne was standing, hackles up, blue eyes staring wildly. "There's a good puss, come on."

But *would* Daphne be helped? No, not on your tail tip, she wouldn't. Like the perverse animal she was, she backed away from her benefactor, hissing horribly.

"Oh, for fur's sake, Daphne, get a grip on yourself," called Marmaduke, irritated by her stupid behaviour. "The man's come to help you."

"Puss, puss, come on puss," called the painter, not sounding quite so patient.

Hiss! Spit! Snarl!

"Oh, to hell with the stupid animal! I haven't got all day," swore the painter, by now thoroughly exasperated.

"Just grab her," called Marmaduke. Then in Miaowpurrese he yowled to Daphne "Put your paw in your mouth, you undignified animal and stop that ridiculous hissing. You're a disgrace to the name of cat."

Finally the man grabbed Daphne by the scruff of her neck, and holding her in one hand and steadying himself on the ladder with the other, he descended to the group below.

"Here you are," he said, handing the still snarling animal to Jenny. "And welcome!"

The words were scarcely out of his mouth when the ungrateful Daphne lashed out at him with her paw.

"Daphne, how *could* you!" exclaimed Jenny in disgust, and dropped her on the ground.

In a second Marmaduke had bounded up and given his feline friend two sharp cuffs across the whiskers.

"That's quite enough, Daphne," he said sternly. "Apologise to this gentleman immediately or we'll put you back on top of your pillar and leave you there for ever."

Marmaduke's sharp rebuke brought the hysterical animal to her senses. She turned to her benefactor and opening wide her big, china-blue eyes she purred ecstatically and came up to rub herself affectionately against his leg.

"Oh thank you, thank you," she purred, "you're the darlingest, most wonderful man, a *purr*fect angel and I'll send you a pawmarked copy of my latest publicity picture. I'm a superstar, you know, a *purr*sonality. But I'll never forget you for your brave deed today. Oh purr, purr, purr!''

"OK, any time," said the man, whose name turned out to be Steve, "but mind those claws in future."

Luckily her unkind scratch had not drawn blood and the painters, children and cats parted the best of friends.

Now everyone wanted to know just how Daphne had got to the top of the pillar and the Siamese was only too eager to tell.

"Well darlings, it was *dreadful*, simply *dreadful*, you've no *idea*," she told them in her best Sloane Ranger miaow. "My agent rang my mistress to say he had this perfectly angelic job for me, something that only a really beautiful and talented cat could do. It's an advert, he said, for highly superior cat food and needs a cat with class, an animal of pedigree. Naturally my name was the first he thought of. Well, one likes to oblige where one can, so I said 'purr' and my mistress agreed.

"But, my dears, *never, never* again. When I get home I'll make my feelings quite plain. Until my mistress rings my agent and tells him how badly I've been treated and that I simply *won't* have another *thing* to do with that organisation, I won't even look at her, let alone purr. 'You're on Top of the World with TOPOCAT' indeed!'' And she snorted with indignation, remembering the slogan that had been responsible for getting her marooned on top of a seven-metre pillar.

"But what happened?" insisted Robert, wanting the facts. "You can't have got up there by yourself."

"Oh no," said Daphne, with a toss of her fine head, "they were all charming at first. My agent rang to confirm the booking and told my mistress 'Darling, your Daphne is just perfect for the job. I've shown the client her publicity pictures and he says she's *absolutely* the one and only because of her *exceptional* good looks.' "

She paused, and then paraded up and down as if on the catwalk at a fashion show, mincing, trotting and finally doing a sort of twist.

"Well darlings," she continued, sweeping her audience with her piercing blue eyes, "they collected me from home just before dawn and we came down here to start filming. One must film early, you understand, to avoid the crowds, especially if one is a superstar. Otherwise there are too many fans about wanting pawmarks. An awful bore but one has to try to please one's public." The children understood what she meant. They had all seen superstars on television chatting about their busy lives.

By now other tourists and shoppers, curious to see what was going on, had gathered in the garden. "What a beautiful cat!" one lady exclaimed. "What eyes! What whiskers!" Daphne loved nothing better than an admiring audience and, with a polite "brrp" to acknowledge the compliment, she resumed her story.

"They did a few shots of me inspecting the hypocaust – 'Head back, right paw up, tail straight' – you know the sort of thing. 'That's right, darling, face to camera, brush your whiskers, lick your lips' and so on for at least an hour until I was utterly worn out. 'Look lovey,' I said to the cameraman, 'I simply *must* have a saucer break. ACAT rules, you know.' It was in Miaowpurrese, of course, but they knew what I meant."

The children had come to realise over the last few days that cats only spoke human language under Marmaduke's influence. It was very strange. "They didn't seem *awfully* keen on a saucer break," continued

81

Daphne, "but one has one's rights, doesn't one? So I decided to put a back paw down. 'Darlings,' I said with a purr, 'naturally I wouldn't *dream* of complaining but it would be most *awfully* inconvenient, wouldn't it, if animal activists were to sabotage your film just for the sake of a humble saucer of milk?'

"They seemed to get the message all right. The director muttered something rude about superstars but I got my saucer. Watery as watery, my dears, but a saucer for all that. And before I'd even had a chance to fix my face – give my fur a lick, preen my fine whiskers, you know the sort of thing – the director said he wanted me on top of this beastly great pillar.

"He carried me up and, can you imagine, I had to pose there in various Supercat attitudes while some idiot kept repeating, 'You're on Top of the World with TOPOCAT!'

"*No one* could say I was a conceited animal but

honestly, darlings, I was *superb*, simply *superb*. Every take a winner.'' And she did another of her mannequin parade catwalks for the even bigger crowd that had gathered in the garden.

Daphne was in her element. 'Perhaps,' she thought to herself, 'there's a talent spotter among the crowd and I'll be snapped up for a Major Promotion.' She continued: ''The director, a bit of a wimp if you ask me, then said, 'Hang on pussywinks, we'll take a few shots over here and come back to you. Toodle pip!'

''Well, the sun was warm by then so I was quite happy to stay there for a bit and I curled up for a rest. I must have dozed off into a catnap because the next thing I knew a group of blackbirds were laughing their horrid yellow beaks off and I was left alone on top of this perfectly revolting pillar. Well, my dears, imagine, Me, the Superstar, abandoned on a pillar!''

There were a few giggles from the crowd at the thought of this undeniably comic sight but Daphne continued unabashed. ''That's the trouble nowadays, there's absolutely *no* consideration for a cat. Treated like *dogs*, we are. If it hadn't been for Marmaduke and his friends here I might have been on that hateful pillar for weeks and weeks.''

''Like Saint Simon Stylites,'' volunteered Bill, who had been making notes. ''*He* sat on top of a pillar for thirty-seven years.''

''Really?'' exclaimed Daphne, excited. ''Perhaps they'll make *me* a saint. I'd make a good saint, with statues of myself in wayside shrines and my picture for sale in the cathedral. Saint Daphne of Chester. Yes, I'd like that!''

''She'd have to be a bit more humble first,'' whispered Rebecca to Jenny.

''And a bit better tempered too,'' said Jenny.

The two girls started to giggle and Daphne gave

them the most withering look it is possible for any cat to give.

"Well, come on," interrupted Marmaduke, "time's getting on and we've lots to do. We're going to see what the Rows looked like a hundred years ago. Are you coming with us, Daphne?"

"Oh, yes, purr," said Daphne, and off they all went.

The reconstruction of the Rows was uncanny. Even the old street noises had been recreated. There was the chemist's shop with its array of mysterious coloured bottles, all neatly labelled with Latin names, the sweetshop, the haberdasher's, the blacksmith's. But what Daphne most wanted them to see was the cat. She was so life-like that Rebecca went up to stroke her before she realised she was only stuffed.

"My great-great-grandmother," announced Daphne with pride in her purr. "One of the best mousers of her day and an outstanding beauty."

The children looked rather shocked at this revelation.

"Oh, how dreadful!" said Jenny.

"Dreadful? Not at all," countered Daphne, bewildered by their squeamishness. "It's a great honour. The taxidermist did a magnificent job. She died young, you know, my great-great-grandmother, just as these Rows were being made and they thought it would be a good idea to preserve her for ever, so that everyone would be able to see how beautiful she was. I'm not a conceited animal" – she licked her fur – "but there never was such a beautiful cat until myself. It's only right and proper she should be preserved."

"Oh, I see," said Jenny. But she didn't really. It seemed rather indecent to have your great-great-grandmother stuffed and put in a museum.

It was now time for tea with Marmaduke's family so

they all made their way down to the River Dee where Mr and Mrs Roberts, Ceri, David and baby Daniel were waiting. Cats are most hospitable animals and the Chester cats were no exception. They, too, had prepared a magnificent feast with the local specialities: Cheshire cheese, and Farndon strawberries, as well as scones, cream and strawberry jam for Joe.

Marmaduke was overjoyed at seeing his family again and ran to greet them with loud purrs.

"Oh, we have missed you so," said Ceri, stroking his thick ginger fur.

"Thanks for the postcard," said David. "I wasn't really sure if you could write."

Marmaduke decided to ignore this last remark. Unable to write, indeed! Why did humans, even young ones, think they had a monopoly on all the intellectual skills? He went over to say purr to Daniel, making sure to get out of the way quickly in case he got his tail pulled.

He turned to introduce everyone but found there was no need. For a moment no one was taking any notice of him. They all seemed to be making friends, the grown-ups talking, the children playing. 'Well,' he thought, 'let the humans talk to each other!' And he strolled down to the edge of the river, where he stretched himself out on the warm paving stones for a short catnap. But in spite of the sunshine and the pleasures of the afternoon, his dream was disturbing.

His whiskers twitched. He was in a cage at what seemed to be a zoo. Catalonian Carmen was pointing at him with an umbrella and saying "Beware, beware", and all about his family and his new young friends were crying and calling "Marmaduke, where are you? Marmaduke!" He kept miaowing "I'm here," but no one could see him or hear him.

85

It was obvious they were going to give up and go away and he would be trapped wherever it was for ever.

"Marmaduke!" Jenny's voice woke him from his sleep with a start. "I've brought you a saucer of milk. Mrs Roberts said you should have one every day to make your whiskers curl. And here are some pilchards in tomato sauce. I thought they might all go."

"Very kind of you, purr!"

"I've made friends with Ceri and so has Rebecca and we've all swopped addresses and telephone numbers. We've had a wonderful day."

Marmaduke was so pleased he had helped make this shy little girl happy that he purred loudly. He would trust her with his life. He wasn't so sure about her father, though. Why was he behaving so oddly, he wondered? One minute he had been saying how much he was enjoying the holiday and now he hadn't a good word for it. And what was Mr Sqynt up to, making all those telephone calls? Why were human beings so complicated?

"I hate historic cities," said Mr Copplestone who had rejoined his wife. "When are we going?" For an instant, when Linda had introduced him to Mr and Mrs Roberts, he had had a fleeting pang of conscience about what he planned to do with their cat, but the image that quickly appeared in his mind of the Witch of Wookey, with her greedy, glinting eyes, had soon put a stop to that.

As it happened, it was time to go just then. Goodbyes were said with promises to meet again soon and the Catspots party made their way back to Joe's coach. Passing a telephone box, they were not surprised to see Mr Sqynt emerge, black briefcase in hand.

"Wrong number?" asked Bill innocently, with a wink at the others.

"Yes, funny that," said Mr Sqynt.

Chapter Seven

CREAM OF MOUSE SOUP

"TODAY," said Marmaduke as his party settled down in the coach, "we are going to my country, Wales. The Honourable Society of Cheshire Cats has kindly invited us all to a banquet by the seaside."

"Can we swim?" "Is there a pier?" "Mum, have you got our buckets and spades?" The children were all talking at once.

"Why," asked Bill, when the commotion had died down, "are the Cheshire Cats giving a banquet in Wales and not Cheshire?"

"Well, for one thing Cheshire hasn't got any real sea," said Marmaduke, "and for another Llandudno, where we are going, is very special to Cheshire Cats because the author who made *the* Cheshire Cat famous in his book *Alice in Wonderland* used to go there for his holidays."

"See what I mean," whispered Mr Copplestone to Mr Sqynt (they always sat next to each other now), "he *is* the Cheshire Cat whatever he says about being from that village with the unpronounceable name. We've got it made."

"What was the author Lewis Carroll's real name?" asked Bill. "The Reverend something or other?"

"The Reverend Charles Lutwidge Dodgson," Marmaduke told him. "He used to stay in Llandudno with the *real* Alice and her family, the Liddells, in their holiday house by the Great Orme."

"What's that?" asked Angus.

"It's a big rocky headland, almost a mountain, that juts out into the sea," he explained. "And it's the place the Cheshire Cats have chosen for their banquet."

"How do we get up there?" asked Robert.

"You'll see," said Marmaduke. "But, look, we're crossing the border into a new country. See the signs, '*Croeso i Gymru*', 'Welcome to Wales'. You say Llan*did*no, not *dud*no, by the way," he continued. "That's the Welsh pronunciation. It means the parish of Tudno, a saint who lived here in the sixth century."

"Could there be a town Llandaphne then, if Daphne became a saint?" asked Robert.

"I don't see why not," purred Marmaduke. He was glad they had all taken to Daphne in spite of her affected ways.

There were plenty of amusements in Llandudno; donkey rides on the beach, Punch and Judy, a pier, and Alice's own Wonderland. Finally, Marmaduke took them to the cable car lift which hoisted them high above the town to the summit of the Orme.

There, on a bank sheltered from the wind, the Cheshire Cats had spread out picnic rugs and on each one lay an elegantly printed menu showing a picture of the Cheshire Cat, grinning.

"Take your places," said Marmaduke. "You are in for a real treat."

They sat down, and within seconds from behind a large rock, eight beautifully groomed cats emerged. Their fur was black, except for snow-white spats and snow-white waistcoats, and round their necks each wore a starched black bow-tie. They moved smartly along on their hind legs, right paws raised to hold aloft impressive silver trays that carried the first course, Sea Food Platter with Salad.

Marmaduke never stood on ceremony where food was concerned and his nose was soon buried deep in his saucer of sardines, smoked salmon and pilchards.

He was just settling his digestive juices with some greenery when he became aware that not everyone was quite as happy with the first course as he.

"But Marmaduke, this is just ordinary *grass* they've mixed with the fish, not lettuce," said Mrs Friendly. "If I had realised they were going to serve grass I would have brought my picnic basket. I hardly ever go anywhere without it."

"We can't be expected to eat *this*!" protested an elderly gentleman.

"I hope they washed it first. You never know *what* may have got onto grass . . ." said a woman. "Ugh!"

"More waste of money," grumbled Mr Copplestone.

"Disgusting!" said Mr Sqynt. "Wouldn't give it to a dog."

Even the children looked dismayed.

"Look," said Marmaduke, trying to lick the tip of

his nose that had got covered in tomato sauce, "there's nothing wrong with grass. It's the best digestive know to cat. And of *course* it's been washed. By the rain."

"By the rain! Acid rain!" said Jenny's mother with horror. She had read all about the destructive properties of rainfall. "You had better not eat it, darling. You don't want to be ill again."

A thick ruff of ginger fur had risen on the back of Marmaduke's neck and his tail lashed slowly. A dissatisfied mutter arose from the party. Jenny felt upset for her friend.

"Never mind, Marmaduke," she said kindly, trying to smooth the ruffled fur, "it's just that humans don't *usually* eat grass. I'm sure the next course will be lovely."

But not everyone was of that opinion, either. Marmaduke's clients were studying their menus with growing puzzlement and consternation.

"*Crème de Souris*. What on earth's that?" demanded Mr Copplestone.

"*Alouette rôtie aux fines herbes*. Oh Marmaduke, if it's what I *think* it is I couldn't possibly eat *that*, not even for *you*," said Mrs Friendly, going a pale shade of green.

"Pait de foy musseragny. Fromidge sour ice. Got me there, Marmie, with your foreign lingo," said Mr Sqynt. "What do these cats charge anyway? Bit of a swiz, bit of a cheat, serving grass. And now sour ice, is it? Sour cream's bad enough but sour ice . . ."

Dan and Ben, who were from the French-speaking part of Canada, looked at Mr Sqynt in surprise. Then Dan laughed, "Oh, you mean *pâté de foie musaraigne*, shrew-mouse liver pate, and *fromage souricière*, mousetrap cheese."

"If you're so clever, tell us what this cream thing is then, and the rotten herb concoction. Sounds like

91

something the cat dragged home. Rather good that, don't you think? Something the cat dragged home. Haw, haw, haw.'' And Mr Sqynt, carried away by his own joke, dug Dan in the ribs.

"Ouch, be careful Arch,'' cried Dan, moving away quickly. "Yes, I'll tell you. *Crème de souris* is cream of mouse soup and *alouette rôtie aux fines herbes* is just what I think Mrs Friendly feared it was - roast lark with herbs.''

"I feel sick,'' said Rebecca.

"Come on, darling,'' said her mother. "We'll go and find a nice café instead with chips and baked beans and cheese on toast.''

The other diners seemed to have the same idea and were all getting to their feet preparing to go, grumbling and exclaiming to each other "Cream of mouse soup, indeed!'' "A right dog's dinner!'' "Thought they'd get away with it, putting it all in French. What do they take us for, a load of ignoramuses?'' "It's a disgrace, that's what it is!'' "Cats!''

The children were upset for Marmaduke and the Cheshire Cats, who, alarmed by the humans' protests, had all got down off their hind legs, removed their bow ties and were huddled, just like any ordinary bunch of frightened cats, behind their rock. Some had even scampered off, tails flying, in case any guest - as humans sometimes do - took to throwing weighty objects. Robert Friendly was the first to speak up.

"How can you say you *don't* like mouse soup, Mum, when you've never even *tried* it? Give the cats a chance. They've gone to so much trouble.''

"I suppose we eat duck and pheasant, so what's wrong with lark?'' asked Bill, not very convinced but trying his best to be fair.

"And there's nothing odd about mousetrap cheese,'' added Angus. "We get *that* all the time at school.''

92

"No, I'm afraid, Marmaduke, you've gone too far this time," said Mr Friendly, taking the lead. "Perhaps you could explain our human tastes to the Cheshire Cats and tell them we're sorry but we really can't eat this. Isn't there anywhere else you can suggest?"

"Well, there's the Mi-Ow Oriental Restaurant run by two Siamese friends of mine. Distant relations of Daphne's in fact. Perhaps we'd better go there," said Marmaduke, crestfallen. He was unhappy, too, at having hurt the feelings of the Cheshire Cats, especially since he was the one responsible for having accepted their kind invitation.

"Well, all right" agreed Mr Friendly, "but no mouse chop suey, mind."

"Oh no," Marmaduke assured him, "they cater specially for human tastes unless otherwise requested."

"They'd better," said Mr Copplestone, "or I for one will want my money back."

"Could be complaints, Marmie old cat," added Mr Sqynt. "Not from me, of course, not from your old pal Arch. But a bit of a call to a newspaper, bit of a letter to a member of parliament, bit of a word to the Environmental Health, like, and goodbye Catspots."

"That's most unjust, Mr Sqynt," protested Marmaduke.

"Arch, call me Arch. Arch by name and . . ."

"All right, Arch," growled Marmaduke, scarcely able to contain himself.

"A joke's a joke, Marmie. No one takes a joke better than Arch. Bit of a wag myself, eh? eh? But mouse soup . . ."

"Come on now, Arch," said Mr Friendly, always one for pouring oil on troubled waters, "I know it's not to our taste but he was only trying to do what the Catspots brochure promised and give us a holiday with a real cat flavour.''

"I'm going to be sick," announced Rebecca. And this time she was.

The situation was saved from disaster by a trip back to the town in the special mountain tramcar followed by a beautiful meal, quite acceptable to the human palate, at Mi and Ow's Oriental Restaurant.

It was so good, in fact, that the next day, when Marmaduke had nothing special planned, the Friendly family decided, along with Jenny and her mother, to go back. But when they reached the spot where they thought the restaurant had been it was boarded up and derelict.

"Look," cried Jenny, "there are Mi and Ow!" And she pointed as two sleek Siamese cats rounded the corner.

"Mi! Ow!" her mother called. "What's happened to your restaurant? We'd like to have some lunch - the food was so delicious."

But instead of advancing with the polite bows and miaows of the day before the two cats turned tail and fled.

"Well, I'll be blowed," said Mr Friendly. "I could have sworn those were the same two cats and that this is the restaurant. I'm seldom wrong about location, am I?"

"No *cariad*, you're not" agreed his wife. "It's very odd."

"Perhaps we dreamed it all," said Jenny sadly.

"We couldn't *all* have had the same dream," argued Robert, the practical one, but he couldn't explain it either.

"Then it must be something to do with Marmaduke," said Rebecca.

"That's right," said Jenny. "We've noticed it

before. These things only happen when we're with him."

"Yes," said Robert, "if we see cats and we're not with him they never take the slightest notice of us or talk or do anything at all out of the ordinary."

"Even Daphne, do you remember, said she spoke to the film crew in Miaowpurrese," Angus reminded them.

"And that whole conversation with her agent was conducted not by Daphne but by her mistress," added Bill. "Marmaduke seems to be the catalyst, if that's the right word."

"It's just the right word," said Mr Friendly. "Certainly he's an amazing animal. I hope he never gets into the wrong hands. There are people who would exploit an animal like that."

A dreadful thought crossed Jenny's mind. Could all this funny talk between her father and Mr Sqynt have something to do with Marmaduke? Surely not.

"Are you all right, darling?" asked her mother. "You've gone quite pale."

"Yes, I'm fine," said Jenny.

Chapter Eight

THE DAWN CHORUS

FROM Llandudno Marmaduke's party went on to stay in a great red castle, Ruthin Castle, where there were deep dungeons to explore. From the ruined battlements peacocks called.

"In a way we're in another country now," said Marmaduke, "the part of Wales that's called Glyndŵr Country, after the Welsh prince Owain Glyndŵr who ruled here in the fifteenth century. My home's not far away and it's my favourite place in the world."

"It's my home too," said Rhiannon Friendly, "*fy nghartref i*. It's lovely to come back."

After a couple of days exploring and meeting the local cats, Marmaduke announced "Early bed tonight. We leave at five in the morning."

"Good heavens, what on earth goes on at that time?" asked Linda Copplestone.

"It's your Special Unusual Treat,"said Marmaduke, purring quietly. "A concert of the Dawn Chorus in the Forest."

"Did you hear that?" whispered Mr Sqynt to Mr Copplestone. "We're going to a forest. This will be my big chance. Bit of luck there, eh, eh?" And he dug Mr Copplestone in the ribs.

"Do you mind?" said his partner in crime.

Later, when they were out of earshot of the others, Mr Copplestone spoke severely. "No bungling this time. We can't afford any more mistakes. Have you got that friend of yours organised for transport?"

"My mate Ronald, yes, he's OK. He'll be there. Doesn't know what the merchandise is, mind. Got to be a bit cautious, a bit canny, a bit prudent, like.''

"Yes, yes," said Mr Copplestone impatiently. "But no mistakes. Meanwhile I'll make arrangements for reception the other end."

Following Marmaduke's advice, everyone except Mr Sqynt and Mr Copplestone went to bed early. Jenny was just getting into bed when she realised she had left her book downstairs. She dressed quickly and went back to the chair in which she had been sitting. There, tucked down the side, was the book. Thank goodness. She ran back towards the stairs and stopped in her tracks. From the telephone box in the hall came the sound of her father's voice. Eavesdropping was not in her nature but this time she felt compelled to listen.

"Is that the office of QE2?" inquired Mr Copplestone. "Good to know some people in this God-foresaken country work all hours. Right. Copplestone here. I have three tickets booked for next week's sailing to New York. That's right, Copplestone; C for cat, O for ordinary, P for purr, P for purr, L for lunatic, E for envy, Stone as in rock. Have you got that? Right. I've got a special parcel arriving to be registered as freight. Can you make sure it's stored properly? What's its category? Oh, I don't know; feline, I suppose. How do you *spell* it? Good God, can't you spell anything? F for furry, E for enemy, L for lock, I for imbecile, N for nasty and E for enough. Yes, *enough*. What *I've* just had - *enough*. E for *enough*. Right. Thank you. Goodbye.''

Quickly Jenny dashed for the stairs, which luckily were out of sight of the telephone box. Her father hadn't seen her.

Back in bed, she didn't want to read, nor could she go to sleep. She lay wondering what the conversation had meant. Something feline? Well, that was to do with cats. But freight, on the QE2? Then it couldn't be a live cat. Perhaps it was a soft toy? Something her father had ordered for her so she wouldn't miss Marmaduke so much after their holiday? That would be nice. That was the sort of thing he used to do before he became so peculiar. She had better not say anything in case it was a surprise. But she felt doubtful about it. At last she dozed off, but it was an uneasy sleep.

DAWN breaks at about half past five in early August, and as the first rays of sun peep over the eastern horizon the birds start their hymn of praise and welcome to the awakening day.

The Dawn Chorus concert had been arranged by Marmaduke's fellow courier, Professor Warblemuch, Professor Longclaw's friend and colleague. Mr Charabanc had thought that it would be nice for the two parties to get together at the end of their holiday for this historic event, but knowing cats well, he had written a 'Paws Off' clause into Marmaduke's contract. Marmaduke had promised to be on his best behaviour during the performance and to refrain from attacking any of the choristers.

With great efficiency, Professor Warblemuch had arranged for all the birds of the forest to have nesting lodgings for the night in one particular spot, so that when dawn came there would be an explosion of singing. Such an event had never been witnessed before in the whole world and everyone felt very excited and rather nervous as they waited in the darkened forest for the moment of daybreak.

At last a distant twitter broke the stillness, filtering down to the wondering audience from the topmost pine tree. In a second there was another, then a chirp, then a warble, and soon the whole forest seemed to erupt in a crescendo of joyous sound.

Through a break in the trees the first faint rays of sun illuminated the leafy auditorium. The children drew their breath in amazement as they looked around and saw, literally, millions of birds. The branches of the trees were weighted down with their feathered bodies and as far as the eye could see, on every log, bush and briar, were perched birds of every shape and size. Even a contingent of ravens was there, adding their deep-throated croak.

In the middle, in a clearing, stood Professor Warblemuch, his wild hair streaming out behind him as, baton in hand, he conducted the singers. The song rose in a crescendo of triumph and praise to greet the new day, and then gradually the music faded and with the sound of much flapping the birds took wing and disappeared. The sun's beams grew broader and stronger and it was time to go back to the Red Castle for the second breakfast of the day.

"There's a little bird over there having some difficulty getting off the ground," Marmaduke told his group. "Poor little fellow, I expect he's only just learning to fly. I'll go and give him a helping paw."

"Oh no, you don't!" Professor Warblemuch advanced towards Marmaduke waving his baton sternly. "Oh no, my good and furry friend, paws off this one. I know *your* sort of help. A flick of the paw and that little chap would be down your gullet, not back in his nest where he belongs.

"Oh Marmaduke, you *wouldn't*," said Jenny.

"Oh, but he *would*," said Robert. "Just look at that funny face he's making, sort of sniggering."

"And he's dribbling as well," said Angus. "What about that 'Paws Off' pact I heard you discussing with Professor Longclaw in Oxford and all that guff about a cat's word being his bond?"

"It's a poor world when a cat can't do a good

99

turn without snide remarks from humans still in their
kittenhood,'' said Marmaduke, ginger fur bristling.

Bill, observing Jenny's father and Mr Sqynt deep
in conversation, changed the subject. ''I wonder what
those two are up to?'' he asked. He'd noticed that

since Wookey Hole they'd had a lot to say to each other and yet they seemed unlikely friends.

But by now everyone's attention was centred on Professor Warblemuch, who was explaining the meanings of different birdsong. "They've got a wide vocabulary," he was saying, "if you just take the trouble to listen."

Marmaduke wasn't interested. It was bad enough having to suppress his hunting instincts without having to listen to an interpretation of what his would-be victims might be saying as well. He stretched himself out on a fallen log in the pleasantly warm rays of the early sun and purred quietly.

"I've just found a nest with some young blackbirds in it." Mr Sqynt had come up beside him. "Fancy a bit of a walk, bit of a promenade, bit of a stroll like? Lovely morning for it, eh, eh?"

"How thoughtful, Arch," said Marmaduke with a polite 'brrrp', "I don't mind if I do." Perhaps Mr Sqynt wasn't so bad after all. Nice of him to think he might be interested in young blackbirds. He licked his lips. 'Well, no harm in just looking,' he said to himself.

The two set off into the forest.

"This way," said Mr Sqynt, and he plunged into a thicket.

"Ouch, ouch, bother that bramble. Ouch, help me, I'm stuck!"

Suddenly Marmaduke remembered the words of Catalonian Carmen. "You have an enemy. Beware the mystery in the thorny bush." Could this be it? Could it be a trap? He approached cautiously.

"What's the *matter* with you?" yelled Mr Sqynt. "Can't you see I'm stuck? Ouch, my hair's caught. Now I've torn my smart jacket!"

Marmaduke wasn't sure that 'smart' was the right

way to describe the dingy brown jacket that Mr Sqynt had worn for every day of the holiday but, certainly, he did appear to be caught in the brambles. How nasty and unjust to have suspected his intentions. Poor Mr Sqynt! He went forward to give a helping paw.

Mr Sqynt's struggles had not improved the situation. Now the brambles seemed to have hold of every bit of his clothing and his face was scratched. His arm was still sore from the scratch Marmaduke had unwittingly given him in the Ghost Train. He was sick of this holiday, sick of everything. "Do something, can't you," he said, "or I'll be here forever?"

Marmaduke was doing something. He had freed a leg but he couldn't reach Mr Sqynt's shoulders and head. "I'll have to get help," he said. "Wait there, I'll be back soon."

"Wait here!" said Mr Sqynt. "That's a stupid thing to say. I haven't got much choice, have I?"

He was particularly angry with himself as the blackbird story had, of course, been a decoy. He had intended, when they got far enough away from the others, to pounce on Marmaduke, tie him up and deposit him somewhere in a safe place for future collection by his mate Ronald. What on earth would Mr Copplestone say now? This was the second time he had made a mess of things. 'That cat leads a charmed life,' he thought. 'Must be the four-leafed clover marking on his nose, bother him.' Out loud he yelled, "Ouch, ouch. Help me! I'll be eaten by wild animals if you leave me here much longer. Help! Help!"

Soon Marmaduke was back with his gang of helpers: all five of the children, plus the two student vets. At last they freed Mr Sqynt, but not without damage to his jacket. "There's a tear in my lovely jacket," said

Mr Sqynt. "Trust you lot! You might have been a bit more careful. Cost me a bomb, that jacket. I'll want compensation, mind you."

"That's not very grateful, Mr Sqynt," said Marmaduke. "We did our best and it wasn't our fault you got stuck in the brambles."

"Arch, if you please, Marmie. Arch by name and Arch by . . ."

"Oh, all right, Arch," said Marmaduke. "Let's get back for that second breakfast. I'm starving!"

Mr Sqynt was a difficult sort of human being, Marmaduke thought to himself as he walked back towards the coach. Thank goodness they weren't all like that! But he had obviously not intended any harm towards him. That warning of Catalonian Carmen's about the thorny bush must have been meant for Mr Sqynt. *He* was the one who had got caught in the brambles. Well, at least it was over and done with. No need to worry about that any more. He sighed.

"Home again soon, eh Marmaduke?" said Mr Friendly, catching up with him. "It's been a marvellous holiday; we've really enjoyed it, all of us. Thank you."

"Yes, I've enjoyed it too," said Marmaduke with a quiet purr, "but it'll be nice to go home."

Little did he realise what terrible adventures lay in store for him before he would see his beloved home and family again.

Chapter Nine

AN UNUSUAL PUSSY WILLOW

IT was the last day of the holiday. Tomorrow Marmaduke would be waving them all goodbye for another year, at least.

He had chosen to end the Catspots Tour in Llangollen, a pretty picture-postcard town on the River Dee in North Wales, where every July people come from all over the world to take part in the International Eisteddfod, a festival of music, dance and song. It was not far from his home village of Pontybodkin.

"The Eisteddfod is not on at the moment," Marmaduke told them, "but to give you an idea of what it's like I've arranged a special concert for you on the Eisteddfod field, known in Welsh as the *maes* and pronounced like that well-loved English word 'mice'." He licked his lips at the thought. "Come on!"

They walked over the old bridge, built, Marmaduke told them, in the fourteenth century, past welcoming cafés and bright, cheerful shops until a slope took them up to the big field. Far above on the mountain top they saw the ruins of Castell Dinas Brân, crows' city castle.

But for the moment their attention was drawn to a curious mound in the middle of the field, a sort of rock, glinting copper and gold in the sun.

"What's that?" asked Robert.

"Wait and see," said Marmaduke, and as he spoke the mound began to move like a bubbling volcano.

"It's erupting," said Angus.

"It's cats," said Bill.

"It's the Purrs of Pontybodkin!" exclaimed Jenny

and Rebecca as one. "What beautiful ginger fur, what lovely long white curling whiskers!"

By now the cats had formed into an orderly group and at a sign from their conductor they burst into exuberant caterwauling.

"Oh we are the Purr Cats,
The Purr Cats of Pontybodkin,
Oh we are the animals
With melodious purr.

"We've got ginger fur and snow-white waistcoats,
And long white curling whiskers,
Lime green eyes, pink noses
And thick bushy tails.

"Oh we are the Purr Cats
The Purr Cats of Pontybodkin,
Oh we are the animals
With melodious purr.

"Our coats are like marmalade,
Our socks are like snowflakes,
Our eyes are like saucers
That gleam in the dark . . . "

"Come on now, all join in the chorus," called Anthony, the conductor, and everybody, even Mr Sqynt, sang the famous lines.

Marmaduke's family was enormous but when the song had finished the children managed to shake paws with most of them.

Jenny was especially pleased to meet Marmaduke's mother, who was very like him apart from not having a four-leafed clover mark on her face.

"You must be very proud of him," said Jenny, stroking her fine ginger fur.

"Oh, I suppose so," she purred, "but really once they are adult I'm not that interested. It's kittens I love."

"May we come and see you one day in Pontybodkin?" asked Bill. He was fascinated by the village and its name.

"Yes, purr," said Marmaduke's mother, "we'd be delighted. It's a little village just over the high moors from here, on the way to Chester, and we live with the Evans family at Bryn Awelon, the breezy hill. Just follow the purring and you'll find us."

"I've never known anyone with so many aunts," said Angus to Robert later when they were discussing Marmaduke's extensive family. "We've only got one and that's your mother, Auntie Rhiannon."

"And he's got *so* many brothers and sisters he can't even remember *how* many," said Rebecca.

"But haven't they got a beautiful purr?" said Jenny, "No wonder they are called Purr Cats. I'll never forget this holiday, ever."

"Come on," called Marmaduke, "we've got more treats in store."

"God knows what we're doing joining in with this rubbish," said Mr Copplestone to Mr Sqynt as they followed Marmaduke and the others at a distance. "Sometimes I think I'm going out of my mind. And *you* don't help."

"Sorry," said Mr Sqynt. Mr Copplestone had been extremely angry with him after the episode in the brambles. "Sorry. But we'll get him this time. Third time lucky, eh, eh?" And he was about to nudge Mr Copplestone in the ribs but restrained himself just in time. He knew how it irritated him.

"It had better be," said Mr Copplestone. "This is

our last chance, our last chance to get rich. Do you realise that, you bungling oaf?"

"Arch, if you don't mind. Arch by name and arch by . . ."

"All right, all right! – Now let's run through the plan again. When you bugged his room last night, you heard him talking on the telephone to that Charabanc person in London, so you know exactly what we will be doing today and where we are going."

"Yes, and I've done a quick recce this morning so I know just the spot to get him. The cat will be in the bag by this afternoon all right. Trust me. Bit of a trickster, bit of a schemer, bit of a plotter. Purr-suer, get that? Purr-suer . . . haw, haw, haw."

"I'm not in the mood for jokes," said Mr Copplestone drily. " – And your mate, Ronald? Has he got his instructions? After that farce in the forest I'm surprised he's ready to stand by again. Not to mention that ridiculous business at Whittington Fair."

"We're paying him well, aren't we?" said Mr Sqynt, aggrieved.

"Not that well, I hope," said Mr Copplestone. Although he was anticipating that before long he would be a millionaire, with his share of the cash Disneyland had promised them for Marmaduke safely stashed away in a Swiss bank, he did not like to waste money. That was not his nature. "You think he'll come with you then? Marmaduke, I mean?" he asked. "He's not suspicious or anything?"

"Not a bit," replied Mr Sqynt. "Came like a lamb other day. Lamb to the slaughter."

'Yes, well don't get carried away. Remember what aid about not damaging the merchandise."

By now the rest of the party had reached the canal, where a barge was waiting to take them on a trip. It

107

was to be pulled by a horse called Harry and he was pawing the ground on the tow path, anxious to be off.

"Come on," called Marmaduke. "Come on, Arch, come on, Mr Copplestone. Don't miss our farewell treat!"

'Little does he know how farewell it is,' thought Mr Copplestone, and he felt a pang of conscience. Surely this was not the way to treat an animal who had been so kind? An image of the Witch of Wookey flashed across his mind and he forgot his conscience.

Harry was a strong horse. Soon they were moving smoothly along the canal, leaving the little town behind. Below them was the Eisteddfod field and there, waving their paws, were the Purr Cats of Pontybodkin. Rebecca began to hum the famous song.

After a bit they pulled up at a quiet spot on the bank.

"This is where we will have our farewell picnic," announced Marmaduke. "Thanks, Harry, for carrying the hampers. Perhaps, Bill and Angus, you could get them down off Harry's back for me?"

This time Marmaduke had taken no risks with the feast and had sought Mrs Friendly's advice on every item. The only extra he had included was a bag of choice oats for Harry. It was a glorious day, sunny but not excessively hot. Though it was late summer, the grass on the mountains was still green and the water in the canal sparkled in the sunlight. To complete feast, Marmaduke and Mrs Friendly had order magnificent cake from the local baker in the sh a ginger cat. Even Harry said he would have though he didn't normally eat cake.

"Right," said Marmaduke, "we'll all be go separate ways soon, so are there any last questi would like to ask on Catistory or Catlore? I'd

108

too happy to oblige.'' He knew that Ben was doing his thesis at university on 'The Role of the Cat in Social History', and he was anxious he should do well.

There were a lot of questions from the adults so the children went off to play. After a time the grown-ups began talking among themselves and Marmaduke lay back in the sun to relax. A light catnap would not be amiss, he thought.

''Sorry to disturb you, Marmie, but could you help me out with a bit of plant identification? A rather unusual pussy willow, as a matter of fact.'' It was Mr Sqynt. ''I'm a bit of a plant lover, bit of a botanist, bit of a gardener, like, but I've never seen anything like this before.''

''I didn't know you were interested in botany, Arch. Yes, certainly I'll help if I can. Where is it?''

''Just over here. Caught my eye as I went for a stroll. Thought to myself, there's only one animal who can solve this: Marmie. Over here. Mind how you go!''

''Yes, we don't want an accident like last time.''

'We certainly do not,' thought Mr Sqynt. He had built all his hopes on this deal with Disneyland. ''Not far now,'' he said.

''It's funny to see a pussy willow in August,'' said Marmaduke. ''They are usually out in early spring.''

''My thoughts exactly,'' said Mr Sqynt. He was ˙athing hard now and seemed very excited. He ˈ't very fit and often got out of breath.

˙ must have found something really unusual,' ˌt Marmaduke, and he hurried forward, rs alert.

ˌ, there it is, in there,'' said Mr Sqynt, pointing ˌck blackberry bush. ''Funny sort of a plant, bit ˌkin, bit of a pussy willow, growing up right in

109

the centre of the bush. A most unusual specimen. Just put your head in and you'll see.''

With his right paw Marmaduke separated some of the brambles and peered into the dark tangle. It *did* just cross his mind that this was another thorny bush. But *that* danger was all in the past now. And it was poor Arch who had been caught, not him. 'Don't be silly,' he said to himself, 'Arch means no harm.'

He was wrong.

"Got yer! Oh no, my furry friend, you don't get away *this* time. *This* time Arch is making no mistakes. Third time lucky!'' And he threw a big net over Marmaduke.

'Third time?' thought Marmaduke. 'So it must have been Arch in the Ghost Train. And when *he* got caught in the forest he must have meant to trap

me instead. But why?' He squirmed and wriggled, his paws flailing wildly, but the more he struggled, the more enmeshed he became.

Mr Sqynt reached for a blanket. He was not going to get scratched this time, oh no. He wrapped Marmaduke, net and all, in it and carried him over to where a sturdy wooden box was waiting. Obviously the whole operation had been carefully planned. So someone *had* been listening in to his phone call to Mr Charabanc the other night. Marmaduke's twitching whiskers had told him that something was wrong. And it must have been Mr Sqynt because the whole treat had been kept a strict secret.

"What on earth . . . what are you doing, Mr Sqynt, I mean Arch?" miaowed Marmaduke wildly. "What do you want? What have I done?"

"Nothing, Marmie old chap, nothing. It's what you *are*, not what you've *done* that matters. *That's* what's going to help your old friend Arch make an honest penny."

"Honest penny? What do you mean? You're not going to sell me, surely?"

"Right first time, Catto. Disneyland, that's where you're going. In California, US of A."

"Disneyland? Why? I'm not a film star. Why should they want *me* there?"

"Oh come now, you can't fool Archibald Sqynt, super snooper. *You're* the Cheshire Cat, the *famous* Cheshire Cat from the old book you told us about. And Georgie Copplestone, my mate, *he* says that Walt Disney, that cartoon maker person, made the book into a film with you as the star."

"That's not me," miaowed Marmaduke, but Mr Sqynt wasn't listening. He was carrying Marmaduke, firmly strapped in his box, towards the road. The noise of traffic grew louder at every step. Oh why

111

hadn't he heeded more the wise words of Catalonian Carmen? Beware the *mystery* in the thorny bush, she had said, not just the thorny bush. And what else was it? 'Beware the place where the water flows in a man-made river.' Of course, the *canal*. Why hadn't he thought of that? 'You have an enemy who is plotting against you. Beware the false friend'. That was Mr Sqynt, of course. He *had* seemed friendly and so interested in plants and wildlife. What a gullible animal he had been to be taken in, and he, a cat of the world!

But hadn't she warned of a second enemy, 'another who has been led astray'? Beware *them*, she had said. Mr Sqynt had called Mr Copplestone his mate. Surely *he* wasn't involved? His behaviour had been very odd since Wookey. It was there that he had suggested the American lecture tour which Marmaduke had turned down and since then he had been most disagreeable. But Jenny's father . . . ?

They had reached the road where a battered old van was parked in a lay-by. By it stood a tall man dressed in tattered jeans and a dirty denim jacket. He was smoking a cigarette that he threw, still alight, into the woods at the side of the road.

"Careful, Ronald, you might start a fire," said Mr Sqynt.

"What do I care?" said Ronald. "I'll be miles away by that time. Got the merchandise then? Third time lucky, eh? This the package?"

"That's it, Ronald. Straight to Southampton and register it as freight," said Mr Sqynt. "It's for that big boat, the QE2. Got it?"

"Leave it to me, Arch. No problem."

The QE2? So it was all true and they *did* mean to take him to America. He heard footsteps. Perhaps help was at hand? He miaowed loudly.

112

"Cat in the bag then, Arch?" It was Mr Copplestone's voice. "Third time lucky, I suppose?"

Marmaduke's worst fears were realised. But at least Mr Copplestone was a good businessman. He could talk to him and he would see sense, surely?

"Please, Mr Copplestone," he called from his box, in what he hoped was a calm and sensible voice, "you've made a terrible mistake. I'm not the Cheshire Cat. He was only a character in a story. Honestly, they just wouldn't want me in Disneyland."

"Of course you're the Cheshire Cat," said Mr Copplestone irritably. "As near as can be, anyway. You live in Chester, don't you? You've got a grin like, well, like a Cheshire cat and you can talk and recite poetry."

"Please believe me, Mr Copplestone," Marmaduke pleaded as he saw his chances of freedom diminishing. "I wasn't even born in Cheshire so I'm not even *a* Cheshire cat, let alone *the* Cheshire Cat. I was born in Wales; my family are the famous Purrs of Pontybodkin. You heard them this morning. Ask any cat and he'll tell you."

"I've no time to go round asking damn fool questions of cats. As far as I'm concerned, you're the Cheshire Cat and if it does for me it will do for Disneyland."

"Quite right, Georgie," said Mr Sqynt. "Don't take any notice of him. And remember, he's going to make us both millionaires."

Marmaduke was wracking his brains for what to say next. At all costs he must stop them from putting him in that van. "There's another thing," he miaowed from his box. "The Cheshire Cat could disappear and re-appear and I can't do that *and* he was tabby while I am ginger."

Mr Copplestone was uneasy. He didn't think being

ginger mattered too much (something furry with a few stripes would do) but he had forgotten about the Cheshire Cat's ability to disappear at will.

Mr Sqynt provided the answer. "If he could disappear Disneyland wouldn't want him at all because then no one could see him. So it's just as well he can't. We couldn't sell them an invisible cat, eh Georgie, eh?"

That seemed reasonable enough and anyway Mr Copplestone was tired of arguing. "These are just excuses," he said. "Let's get it over with."

Marmaduke made one last attempt. "Mr Copplestone, if you sell me in the United States I shall be too unhappy to smile and I shall refuse to talk. No one will want to pay money to see a perfectly ordinary ginger cat." (For a moment, for the first and perhaps the last time in his life, Marmaduke thought of the Purrs of Pontybodkin as perfectly ordinary.) "Everyone knows that animals, and cats in particular, will not, indeed cannot, perform tricks if they are unhappy. You won't be able to force me to talk. From now on until you let me go, I won't say another word." With that, Marmaduke settled himself as best he could in his uncomfortable box.

Mr Copplestone was taken aback. For the first time since the visit to Wookey when the desire for great riches had overtaken him, he began to have serious doubts about his action. His conscience had pricked him a couple of times, yes, but he had never really thought of abandoning the project. Now he wondered if Marmaduke was right about unhappy animals. Would he refuse to talk? Or grin, for that matter? What a fool he himself would look then! And what would his wife and Jenny say if they found out what he was doing?

But before he could express any doubt, Mr Sqynt

114

had said "Bung him in the van, Ronald. No need to handle with care, eh, eh?" And he dug Ronald in the ribs with his bony elbow.

Ronald had been listening to this three-way argument in amazement. Now he saw he could be onto a good thing. "Look 'ere, guv.," he said to Mr Copplestone, "I thought it was just a parcel I was taking, an old antique or some such junk. I didn't realise I was getting lumbered with a talking cat. I mean, that's another thing, i'nit? I don't know as 'ow I can see me way to taking a Talking Cat all that way for the same price. After all, he'll need feeding an' watering an' so on."

"All right, all right," said Mr Copplestone. An image of the Witch of Wookey had flashed across his mind and dispelled his misgivings. It was funny how thinking of the Witch always had that effect. "All right," he said again; "fifty pounds now and one hundred when you deliver him safely to me on the ship. I don't want him escaping. If there's any danger of that don't bother to let him out at all. He'll survive, a big, strong cat like that."

Mr Copplestone was not a cruel man but he still seemed to be under an evil spell, as though Someone or Something really nasty was directing his words and actions.

Marmaduke was flung unceremoniously into the back of the van. By now he had managed to get the blanket away from his eyes and he could see a little through the ventilation holes Mr Sqynt had made in the box. But his paws were still hopelessly caught up in the cruel netting. There was no way of escape. He would simply have to wait until Ronald took pity on him and let him out. Then he would make a dash for freedom.

But what if Ronald were too afraid of losing his

115

£100 to risk letting him out at all? It didn't bear thinking of. Marmaduke decided to force himself to catnap so that when the opportunity came he would have the strength to run and, if necessary, fight.

"Well, Operation Marmaduke is on the way," said Mr Copplestone as they watched the van drive off. "Thank goodness for that. Come on, Arch, we had better get back to the others. We don't want to arouse suspicion."

It was such a lovely day that most of the party, even the children, were lying about on the grass, reading, chatting or simply sunbathing. No one had noticed the absence of Mr Sqynt and Mr Copplestone. Or of Marmaduke.

It was Jenny who looked for him first. Her father had hired a car so they could drive that same evening to Southampton in order to be in good time for the sailing the following afternoon. She wanted to say goodbye to Marmaduke and thank him by herself. The holiday had meant so much to her. She had made new friends and was not nearly so afraid of life and people as she had been before.

But where was he? She walked round the various groups, she looked in the barge, she asked Harry if he had seen him. He was nowhere to be found. Soon everyone was looking for him.

"Let's all shout together," suggested Mr Friendly. "One, two, three, MARMADUKE!"

"Maaaaaaaarmaduke," neighed Harry, but there was no answer.

"I hope he didn't fall in the canal," said Rebecca.

"I'm sure he can swim," her mother reassured her. "All cats can, although they don't like water."

Next Mr Friendly organised search parties, in which both Mr Sqynt and Mr Copplestone joined, but Marmaduke was nowhere to be found.

116

"It's obvious what's happened," said Mr Copplestone; "he's reverted to pure cat, and has just gone off, in the way cats do."

"But he wouldn't have gone without saying goodbye," said Jenny.

"No, not Marmaduke,"said the others.

"You think just because he talks and sings and makes jokes that he's like us," said Mr Copplestone. "But he's not, he's an animal. He doesn't have feelings or a sense of duty or a conscience like we do." He felt a terrible pang of remorse as he uttered the words, but a stop had to be put to all this searching.

And he, Linda and Jenny had to be off to Southampton.

"I'm afraid Mr Copplestone may be right. He *is* only an animal when all's said and done," said Mr Friendly. "I think we had better all go back to the hotel. He'll probably turn up later as if nothing had happened."

"We ought to ring his family in Chester, " said Mrs Friendly. "Perhaps he's gone back there."

"And the Evanses in Pontybodkin," added Bill, remembering his conversation with Marmaduke's mother. "He may have rejoined his cat family."

"But not without saying goodbye," said Rebecca, and burst into tears.

As Harry pulled them back up the tow path, he was sobbing too, in the way horses can. He couldn't believe either that Marmaduke would leave without saying goodbye.

When they got back, the car Mr Copplestone had ordered was waiting.

"Arch is coming with us," he told his wife, "so we'll travel in the front and you and Jenny can sit at the back."

"Do we have to take that dreadful man?" said

117

Linda. "Haven't you seen enough of him this holiday? You've hardly spoken to anyone else and you've ignored us."

"Well, I see you two all the time, don't I? Anyway Arch and I have business to attend to. Hurry up or we'll never get there."

It was no use arguing. Goodbyes were said and sadly the children parted company.

"I'll ring you in the morning," said Jenny to Rebecca, "before we get on the boat. Give Marmaduke my love if he comes back and say goodbye for me."

"I will," said Rebecca. "Mummy's keeping in touch with his family in Chester and with Mr and Mrs Evans in Pontybodkin, so we'll know if he's gone to either of his homes and Dad's gone to the police station to report him missing. If he doesn't turn up tonight Joe's promised us we can all go back in the morning and have another search by the canal. He says Mr Charabanc has told him that he can have the coach for as long as he needs it."

"Cheer up, Jenny," said Robert. "We'll do all we can to find him."

"I'll take some pilchards in tomato sauce on the search tomorrow," said Angus. "The smell may attract him."

"And we'll sing the Purr Cats of Pontybodkin song," said Bill. "He's bound to hear that."

Mr Copplestone sounded the horn. "Get in, Jenny, we're late. We've got a long way to go."

The loss of Marmaduke and the parting with her friends was more than Jenny could bear. She burst into floods of tears.

"For goodness sake stop that blubbing," said her father crossly.

"She's only a *child*, George," pleaded her mother.

"Child? She's nine. Plenty of children of nine are out earning a living. It's about time she grew up and stopped living in fairyland. What's she going on about, anyway? He's only a cat."

The journey was not a happy one.

Neither was Marmaduke's. After about three hours of driving Ronald stopped at what Marmaduke supposed must be a motorway café but he never came to see how Marmaduke was or ask whether he wanted a saucer of milk or a bit of stretch-paw. Escape was not going to be easy.

They drove on for about another three hours and finally came to a halt outside a semi-detached house in the suburbs of a big town. Marmaduke heard the back doors of the van being opened and felt himself being lifted out into the now rather chilly night air. He was carried up a path to the front door, which Ronald opened with his own key. This, thought Marmaduke, must be his home. Surely he'll let me out now?

"What's in that box, Ronald? Is it alive?" It was a woman's voice. "I don't want any horrid, smelly animals in here!"

"It's just some mangy cat I've got to take to the docks in the morning," her husband replied. "You'd better get some earth put in a box for it and a saucer of water. Don't want the 'orrible thing dying on us or messing up our nice clean 'ome."

'Mangy cat, indeed!' thought Marmaduke, and his hackles rose at the insult. 'Clean house, ugh! I can smell the dirt from here!' And he put his right paw, which he had managed to free from the net, across his nose to quell the stench of old cigarette ash, dirty laundry and greasy, unwashed pans.

Ronald took him upstairs to a small room. "Right, I suppose I'll 'ave to free you to do your business but no tricks, mind."

Marmaduke was thankful to be rid of the blanket, and even more so of the netting, but he was so fed up and frustrated he couldn't resist lashing out at Ronald with his paw. He got in a nice deep scratch on his cheek. What Ronald said is not printable here.

Once outside the room, he called downstairs to his wife, "Vicious brute nearly scratched me eyes out! I've locked him in the box room."

A minute later Marmaduke heard other footsteps on the stairs. It was Dot, Ronald's wife, bringing his tray of soil.

Marmaduke was ready. As she came in, carrying the tray before her, he bit her smartly on the ankle. She tripped and fell, spilling the earth all over the room.

In a flash he was down the stairs and looking wildly for an open window. There in the front room was his chance, a window, wide open. He leapt through in one bound, his ears ringing with the angry cries of Dot and Ronald.

But Ronald had no intention of losing his charge at this late stage in the game. Snatching a large paperweight from the sideboard he threw it after Marmaduke and caught him right between the ears.

Stars flew before Marmaduke's eyes, he had a brief picture of his family at home in Chester, the people he loved best in the whole world, and then everything went black.

Chapter Ten

CAT OVERBOARD!

IT was another hot day and Mr Copplestone decided
to leave his jacket in the hotel bedroom while he and
his family had breakfast. Their luggage was packed
and waiting in the foyer ready for the short taxi
journey to the QE2 and Mr Sqynt, who had been
staying in cheaper lodgings nearby, had come to see
them off.

"Run upstairs, would you Jenny, and fetch my
jacket?" said her father after breakfast. "It's hanging
up in the wardrobe. Here's the key."

"All right, Daddy," said Jenny. It would be a good
opportunity to ring Rebecca and find out if there had
been any news of Marmaduke. The hotel proprietor in
Llangollen had very kindly told her she could reverse
the charges. She let herself into the big double room
and went to the wardrobe. The wardrobe was big, too,
and Jenny found it quite difficult to reach the jacket
on its hanger. She jumped and grabbed it and it slid
to the floor. Out of the inner pocket fell a document.
She was just about to replace it when she noticed the
title 'Operation Marmaduke'. 'What on earth can this
be?' she thought to herself. 'I know I shouldn't look at
Daddy's papers but . . .'

What she read made her feel quite faint.

'We the undersigned, George Edward Copplestone
and Archibald Josiah Sqynt, being of sound mind, do
hereby declare that we will share, divide or otherwise
distribute in equal parts any sum or sums to be
obtained by the sale, lease or loan of the feline being
known as Marmaduke Purr Cat, presently of Chester,

121

to Disneyland of California, USA. Signed this 20th day of August in the year of Our Lord . . .'

So *that's* what had happened to Marmaduke. Her father and Mr Sqynt had plotted together and catnapped him. What had Mr Friendly said that day in Llandudno? 'There are people who would exploit an animal like that'. It was too horrible to think of. But where was he now? She remembered the telephone conversation she had overheard between her father and the QE2 office that night before the Dawn Chorus concert. He had told them to expect a special parcel to be registered as freight, category feline. It had never occured to her that the parcel could be Marmaduke. But it must be. She must ring Rebecca and tell her.

The operator got through. Rebecca, who had been waiting for her call, answered. "Miss Copplestone calling from Southampton," said the operator. "Will you accept the charge?"

"Yes, yes," said Rebecca.

"Go ahead, caller," said the operator.

"Listen, Rebecca, I haven't got much time but I think I know where Marmaduke is."

"Where? Where?"

"It's awful, but I think Daddy and Mr Sqynt have catnapped him. They've put him on the QE2 to take him to America and sell him to Disneyland." Briefly she told Rebecca about the document 'Operation Marmaduke' and the telephone conversation she had overheard.

"How dreadful!" exclaimed Rebecca. "What can we do?"

"This is my plan," said Jenny. "We're leaving for the ship now. As soon as I get aboard I'll start looking for him and I'll try to rescue him before we set sail. Can you all come down to meet him? I'm sure he's there."

"It certainly looks like it," said Rebecca. "Oh, poor little animal! I knew he wouldn't go without saying goodbye."

"I must go," said Jenny, "or they will be wondering what's happened to me."

"Good luck," said Rebecca.

Everyone was horrified at the news about Marmaduke. They didn't want to believe it, but taking into account the odd behaviour of Mr Copplestone and Mr Sqynt and the discovery of the incriminating document by Jenny, it seemed all too possible. Mrs Friendly rang Mrs Roberts.

"Joe says he'll collect you in Chester and drive us all down to Southampton in the coach," she said. "I'm sure Jenny will find him. Don't worry."

"We'll be ready,' said Mrs Roberts. "I won't be happy until I see his little furry ginger face with the white four-leafed clover mark. He's such a dear, faithful friend."

"*There* you are," said Mrs Friendly, "the four-leafed clover mark. That's lucky. It means he'll be all right, you'll see."

Mrs Roberts set about preparing for the journey. In with the sandwiches and biscuits she put a tin of pilchards in tomato sauce. A large tear dropped onto it and splashed onto the floor.

"Miaow!" It was Daphne. She had called round to see Marmaduke, thinking he would have finished his Catspots tour by now, and was shocked to learn what might have happened to him. "Miaow," she said again, and fixed Mrs Roberts with her great blue eyes.

"She wants to come too," said Ceri. "May she?"

"Of course," said her mother.

But there was something Daphne had to do first. She would just have time. When no one was looking,

123

she grabbed a paper and pencil and wrote a note to the freelance reporter who lived a few doors away. He would know what to do with such an important news story.

'Famous talking ginger cat Marmaduke catnapped for sale in Disneyland, United States,' she wrote. Her writing wasn't nearly as good as Marmaduke's (he had taught her) and she found it very difficult. 'Believed held under duress on QE2, sailing from Southampton this p.m. Big rescue operation planned.' She couldn't resist one last line. 'Prominent among the rescuers is glamorous Siamese friend Daphne, Seal Point, model and mother of four.' How good her picture would look on Page Three of a national newspaper! Even in her distress (and she *was* distressed) she thought of her career. She folded the paper, ran along the road and popped it through the reporter's letterbox. By the time she got back to Marmaduke's house Joe had arrived with the coach.

BACK at the Southampton hotel, Jenny ran downstairs with the jacket to join her parents and Mr Sqynt in the foyer.

"What's kept you so long?" snapped Mr Copplestone. "I want to be on that boat in good time. I've got business to attend to."

"I felt sick," said Jenny, and it was quite true.

"You do look very pale, darling. Are you all right?" asked her mother.

"First it's floods of tears, then she's ill. There's always something the matter," said Mr Copplestone impatiently. "Perhaps you two had better not come with me. I'll cancel your tickets and go by myself. Much less trouble."

"Oh no, I'm much better now," said Jenny quickly. Whatever happened she *had* to get on

124

that boat. Otherwise poor Marmaduke had no hope.

"All right," said her father. "I'm sorry, I'm a bit on edge at the moment." Once again his better nature, his old nature, was trying to reassert itself. He had a pang of conscience about Marmaduke, too. He would transfer him from freight to animals' quarters once he got on board. Was he doing the right thing, he wondered, trying to make all this money out of a harmless cat? An image of the Witch of Wookey flashed across his mind and he knew the answer.

"Best be on your way," said Mr Sqynt. "Remember you've got business to attend to, eh, eh?" And he dug Mr Copplestone in the ribs.

"Quite. Well, goodbye Arch and I'll be in touch."

"Goodbye, Georgie, and remember our deal." Mr Sqynt patted his breast pocket where Jenny could see the top of a document similar to her father's. "Who wants to be a millionaire, eh, Georgie, eh?"

"What does he mean by all that?' asked Linda, relieved to see the back of the nauseating Mr Sqynt.

"Oh nothing," said her husband. "Just a private joke."

WHEN Marmaduke recovered consciousness he was back in his uncomfortable box but the smells around him were quite, quite different. He could smell engines and the sea and there was a lot of shouting and bustling going on.

His head was throbbing from the terrible blow he had received and when he felt with his paw he could hardly believe the enormous lump that had swollen up between his ears.

'Oh, I do hope it goes down before my family, Ceri, David and Daniel see me again,' he thought immediately, his natural - and justifiable - vanity gaining the upper hand even in such terrible circumstances.

The floor on which his box stood seemed to be moving slightly - or was it his woozy condition that made him *think* it was moving?

Then he heard a great hooting sound. It was a siren. Of course, he was on a ship, the QE2, going to America!

He had to get out, and back ashore, before the ship started on her journey or he might never see his home and family again. He scratched frantically at the top of the box and tried to gnaw away the wood round the ventilation holes made by Mr Sqynt. He had strong teeth and if he could make a hole large enough he could escape. But all he succeeded in doing was to knock the box over on its side.

Then he had a brilliant idea, a really Marmadukian idea. Through one of the holes he could just make out a chink of light in the distance.

'That chink must be at the bottom of a door,' he thought, 'and if I knock the box over and over I can get to that door and perhaps attract someone's attention.'

He would then try to persuade whoever was there to open the box and, for the rest, he would chance his luck.

Another long, loud siren. Then, surely? Yes, the great ship was moving. At the rate she would go - some twenty-eight knots, he estimated - they would be out of Southampton Water and in the middle of the ocean in no time at all.

He *must* get out now or all was lost. At best, once he was out of territorial waters he would have to go into quarantine for six months on his return to the UK. He knew all about the danger of rabies and how no animal was allowed to land in Britain without going into strict quarantine. At worst, he might die of starvation and neglect in this miserable, dark hold. But time was passing and soon it would be too late.

While he was wracking his brains about what to do next he heard a voice. He froze, wondering who it might be; someone who might be a friend or a heartless animal-hater? At least it wasn't his cruel captor Mr Copplestone, for it was a child's voice. It came nearer, and then he recognised it. It was Jenny's!

"But I can't understand it," she was saying, "I *know* Daddy's got Marmaduke on board, so if he's not with all the other animals and he's not in our cabin, then he *must* be in the hold with the luggage. He came by special parcel delivery, I know that, to be registered as freight, category feline."

"Category feline, eh?" a man's voice replied. "Don't have many of those in our cargo."

"Could we have a look?" asked Jenny. "Just in case."

"Well, it's not *usual*," said the man. Not for the first time Marmaduke wondered how often humans made that excuse, as if being 'not usual' explained everything. What did it matter, he thought crossly, if a thing was 'not usual' so long as it was important?

"Well, it's not at *all* usual," the man continued, "in fact it's most *irregular*, but I suppose we *could*."

"Oh please, please," pleaded Jenny, and Marmaduke could hear a catch in her voice.

"Miaow, miaow," he called as loud as he was able. "Jenny, miaow, I'm here, I'm here! It's me, Marmaduke Purr Cat, miaow, miaow!" In his distress he was using half human speech and half Miaowpurrese. In his anxiety, after he had uttered his calls for help, it seemed an eternity while he waited anxiously for an answer. But Jenny had heard him.

"Listen, that's him; that's Marmaduke! Oh please, please open the door!"

The steward, who had also been amazed to hear Marmaduke, immediately agreed. As he unlocked and opened the door, Marmaduke's box, which he had managed to propel right across the room, fell at his feet. In a minute Jenny had unfastened it and Marmaduke was purring breathlessly in her arms.

"Thank you, Jenny," he said, between gasping purrs, "I knew you would help me if you could. How did you know I was here?"

Briefly Jenny explained about the phone call and the document. "But why Disneyland?" she said. "You've got nothing to do with Walt Disney films, have you?"

"No, but your father and Mr Sqynt seem to think I'm the Cheshire Cat from *Alice in Wonderland*. That's why Disneyland is prepared to pay hundreds and thousands of dollars for me, perhaps millions."

"But you're a Purr of Pontybodkin in Wales!"

"I told them that, and I told them I'm not a bit like the Cheshire Cat; I'm not even the right colour; but they wouldn't take any notice. Do my family know what's happened? I wouldn't like them to think I had run away."

Jenny told him that they did and that they were on their way to Southampton, together with Joe and the Friendly crowd and the two student vets.

"Oh good, purr!" said Marmaduke. "But we must hurry. I've got to get off this ship."

"Too late for that," said the steward practically. "We've set sail. We'll be a long way from shore by now. Don't make such a fuss. The animal quarters are fantastic, not had a complaint, anyway, in all the ten years I've been serving here."

"I'll get off if I have to jump off," said Marmaduke.

"Come on," said Jenny, "let's get on deck."

"You're mad, both of you,' said the steward in despair. "He can't get off the ship now. You're talking about at least a seventy foot drop to the water. It's suicide!"

But Jenny and Marmaduke weren't listening. They knew they had to get to the open deck.

They were, of course, right at the bottom of the great ship. They ran through one doorway and found themselves in a gymnasium facing a lot of hairy-chested men lifting weights. Out again, up some stairs and in through another door. Immediately they smelt a funny smell - it was the hospital.

"Come on, let's try the lift," said Jenny. "I'm sure we won't see Daddy in there; he and Mummy were on their way to the bar when I left them."

They pressed the button marked 'Quarter', the top one in that particular lift, and the next thing they knew they were in an elegant restaurant. The appetising aromas reminded Marmaduke that he hadn't eaten for at least twenty-four hours. He wondered if he dare risk a quick flick of the paw to hook a lamb cutlet from one of the steaming dishes but commonsense got the better of him and he restrained himself. He did not want to be arrested.

Through the restaurant they ran, to the amazement of both diners and waiters, then out, up some more steps, through another doorway and found themselves in a theatre. All these cul-de-sacs were like a labyrinth in a nightmare. preventing them from reaching the open air.

"Oh, my white paws and ginger tail!" exclaimed Marmaduke, "It's bigger than London! won't we *ever* find the deck?"

They ran on, past the library, through a shopping

precinct and then, there above them, was the open deck.

They could still see Southampton, but looking the other way, down Southampton Water, the Isle of Wight seemed unpleasantly close.

The drop from deck to sea was horrific; two or even three times the height of an average house.

"It's no good, I've got to try," said Marmaduke. "Goodbye, Jenny, and thank you for everything!"

A lady passenger was walking towards him, carrying a furled umbrella. Some voice inside him told him to grab it, which, much to the lady's amazement, he did. Jenny threw him a lifebelt, and clutching that in one paw and the now unfurled multi-coloured umbrella in the other, he leapt over the side of the majestic liner.

The brolly acted as a parachute and as he descended towards the churning sea he saw the sun blazing high in the sky above him. Suddenly, in a flash of understanding, Catalonian Carmen's words at Whittington Fair came back to him. "You can be saved. You must seize the bright umbrella and open it in the blazing sun." He had thought it all so silly at the time but how right Catolonian Carmen with her ESP whiskers has been!

"Cat overboard!" the cry went up.

"Stop, thief!" called the lady, whose umbrella had been made to serve such a useful purpose.

Hearing the din, Jenny's parents came out of the bar to see what was going on.

"Man overboard, is it?" asked Mr Copplestone.

"No, cat," someone told him. "Parachuted down on a lady's umbrella. Amazing."

"Well, he'll lose all his nine lives at one go in that lot," another passenger remarked wrily, observing the turbulence the great engines were creating in the backwash below.

"Not a hope," said another. "Poor, demented animal!"

"What sort of cat was he?" asked Mr Copplestone, greatly alarmed.

"Dunno, sort of splodgy," said an informant.

"He was ginger," volunteered a small boy, who had seen the whole fantastic episode, "with a white waistcoat and white paws and a sort of white four-leafed clover mark on his face."

"Oh, my God!" groaned Mr Copplestone. "There goes my fortune. The stupid, stupid animal!" Yet at the same time, to his surprise, he had a feeling of relief, exhiliration almost. His mind felt clear, his limbs felt free. For days now, since Wookey in fact, he hadn't been able to think of anything but making money. The thought had obsessed him day and night and had made his joints ache and his stomach turn over. He had been irritated by anyone or anything not connected with his money-making scheme. Sometimes he had questioned his actions but the vision of the Witch of Wookey that seemed to come before him on these occasions quickly blotted out his conscience. Now the thought of her revolted him. And how had he got into partnership with an unscrupulous villain like Archibald Sqynt? Suddenly he was horrified by what he had done and by the way he had treated his wife and Jenny. He must make amends for the things he has done by saving Marmaduke and restoring him to his family.

"Look!" called the boy who had so diligently observed Marmaduke. "Look! There he is!"

Sure enough, from beneath the foam a bedraggled ginger head emerged, ears flattened, mouth open and gasping for breath. Then, a few feet ahead of him, up bobbed the multi-coloured umbrella. The lifebelt, which he had let fall in his swift descent, appeared only a paw-length or so away on the crest of a wave.

"Catch hold of the lifebelt," called a bewhiskered gentleman, who was following the events with interest. "Bravo, he's got it! He'll be all right now. Fantastic!

132

I wonder why he jumped? Must be desperate to get away from something. Good luck to him, I say!''

By this time nearly all of the 1,815 passengers had crowded onto the various decks to watch the excitement. Most of the 1,000-strong crew seemed to be there as well.

''Stop the ship!'' Mr Copplestone ordered one of the officers. ''Launch the lifeboat!''

''For a cat? Are you mad?'' replied the officer. ''You can't expect us to stop a 66,851-ton vessel mid-ocean for the sake of a mere *cat*.''

''Show me to the Captain!'' ordered Mr Copplestone. ''I've got to save that cat!''

The officer led him up to the bridge. The Captain was polite but firm.

''I'm sorry, Sir,'' he said, ''but I really can't stop my ship to rescue a cat. I've a schedule to keep and, as I'm sure you'll appreciate, my passengers pay a lot of money for the voyage and they expect efficient time-keeping. Anyway, I gather from the purser that you've got no boarding licence for this animal. He shouldn't have been on board at all.''

Deflated, Mr Copplestone returned to the deck. Marmaduke had grabbed the lifebelt, yes, but how long could he survive in the open sea, so far from the shore, without a rescue? He felt utterly dejected and full of remorse. A harmless cat, whose only wish had been to help people and give them pleasure, could be drowned out there and all because he, George Copplestone, had been mad about money. Money-mad. Obsessed with greed.

Jenny was standing gripping the deck rail, tears streaming down her face. Below, some distance now from the ship, Marmaduke struggled in the waves, clinging to his lifebelt with one paw and swimming with the other. The umbrella still bobbed paw-lengths

133

away. At last he got near it, and hooking his claws round the crook, he managed to pull it towards himself. Then, tipping it end-up, he made a little boat and clambered gratefully aboard. Although he was a big cat the umbrella just bore his weight. Now, if he could only find a sail, he might be able to make it back to the dockside.

As if in answer to his cat-prayer, a dolphin appeared alongside the makeshift vessel.

"Did you say you wanted a sail?" asked the dolphin in a highly conversational manner.

"Well, I didn't exactly *say* anything," replied Marmaduke, "but, yes, I *would* like a sail. Have you got one?"

"Just a tick," said the dolphin, and a few seconds later he appeared with a bit of sailcloth and some rope.

Dolphins are amazingly intelligent. Some say they can read thoughts and it seems as though, on this occasion, it was true.

"I'll give you a tow for a bit," said the dolphin, whose name was Adolphus, "then, when you get nearer the quay, you can take yourself in using the sail. With this warm breeze it'll be dry before you can say 'Salmon and Sea-snails!' "

"Did you see that?" said Mr Copplestone, joining his daughter at the ship's side. "He'll be all right now that a dolphin is helping him. What a relief! He can go back to his family."

"But I thought, I thought . . ." began Jenny.

"Yes, I know. You thought Mr Sqynt and I had catnapped him. Well, you were right and I can't say how sorry I am. I don't know what got into me. I thought I could make a fortune by selling him to Disneyland as the Cheshire Cat . . ."

"But he's a Purr of Pontybodkin."

"I know," said her father, "but somehow once the

idea had gripped me, that didn't seem to matter. I thought no one in America would know the difference between North Wales and Cheshire. I was ready to go into partnership with Sqynt, exploit Marmaduke and defraud Disneyland, and all for what? It started in that cave at Wookey when I looked at the Witch. It is almost as though since then I've been under a spell, a spell of greed.''

"Wookey!" said Jenny with a shudder. "It's funny, that's what Angus said when he saw her horrid, glinting eyes. Greed. And we all felt the same.''

"Then Sqynt approached me with his catnapping scheme and things just went on from there.''

Jenny was straining her eyes to see what was happening to Marmaduke, who was now scarcely more than a ginger speck in the distance. "Poor little animal! Will he get there, will he be all right?''

"Would you care to borrow my binoculars, little girl?'' said the gentleman with the beard, who earlier had cheered Marmaduke on. "You'll be able to see everything through them. He's almost home and dry now.''

"Oh, thank you,'' said Jenny.

"Most kind of you,'' said her father.

Through the powerful binoculars, Jenny saw Marmaduke wave goodbye to Adolphus and set sail for the dockside. Next she saw him abandon his 'umbrella boat' and his lifebelt and climb up a rope ladder to the quay. And there, waiting for him, were his family, Mr and Mrs Roberts, Ceri, David and baby Daniel, together with Daphne, Mr Augustus Charabanc, Professor Warblemuch, Joe the driver and all his special friends from the holiday, Mr and Mrs Friendly, Robert, Rebecca, Bill, Angus, Dan and Ben.

"Goodbye, Marmaduke,'' Jenny called, "I'll come

and see you when I get back, I promise.'' Normally her words would have been lost on the wind but a group of friendly seagulls, who had been following the drama, relayed them back in squawks to the quay.

"Goodbye, Jenny,'' called Marmaduke, waving a paw, "and thank you!''

The ship turned course and the quay was lost to sight. Sadly she returned the binoculars to the bewhiskered gentleman. "Thank you so much,'' she said. "I love that animal.''

"I know,'' he said, "I had a cat like that once. My best friend.''

"Oh, there you are,'' said Linda Copplestone, coming up to them. "I lost you in the crowd. Was it Marmaduke and is he all right? How did he get here?''

Her husband and Jenny took it in turns to explain.

"So can we forgive and forget,'' said Mr Copplestone, "and be happy together like we were before, before Wookey?''

"Of course,'' said Jenny and her mother in unison.

"And when we get home, Jenny, perhaps you would like a kitten of your own? After meeting Marmaduke and his friends I've changed my mind about cats. They are splendid animals, highly intelligent.''

"Oh yes, please!''

"What will it be; Persian, Siamese, Burmese?''

"No,'' said Jenny, "just an ordinary ginger one like Marmaduke,'' though she knew as she said it that Marmaduke was in no way ordinary.

"Right, a ginger one it is,'' said her father. "With a white waistcoat and white paws.''

It was wonderful to have her father back to normal again. He had always been kind, in spite of his busy life and business commitments. That's why his behaviour after Wookey had been so hurtful. Now he even approved of cats! How lovely it would be to have a ginger kitten of her very own, perhaps a Purr of Pontybodkin. She started humming the famous song and her parents joined in. It was going to be a lovely trip to America after all.

BACK on the quay, Marmaduke greeted all his human friends in turn with a wet rub of his cheek to their legs. With Daphne, he rubbed noses. But who were all these other people milling around with notebooks and microphones and cameras?

"Take One, Cat," he heard someone call, and a clapper board clapped. A microphone was thrust before his nose. Cameras whirred.

"Tell me, Mr Cat, how did you feel as you jumped from the QE2?"

"Do you always carry an umbrella?"

"Do you do this sort of thing often?"

"Are you a stunt cat?"

'Well, of all the stupid questions!' thought Marmaduke. 'Perhaps it's time I went back to being an ordinary cat.'

But for Daphne's sake (he learned she had given the tip-off to the media), he thought he had better make a bit of an effort to co-operate. He decided, though, not to say anything in human speech. It might be misinterpreted and he didn't want Jenny's father hurt. Somehow, in spite of everything, he knew he wasn't really bad. The Witch of Wookey had no doubt bewitched him and the devious Mr Sqynt had taken advantage.

"Could we just have a picture of the two of you together, you and Daphne? Yes, that's right, cheek to cheek," said a photographer. "And now one of you, Daphne, on your own. That's right, on your hind legs, right paw behind left ear, whiskers up.

Hold it there. Lovely!" Daphne was enjoying herself enormously.

"Will you be preferring catnapping charges, Mr Cat?" asked a reporter.

"Purr."

"You mean you weren't catnapped?" demanded another.

"Purr."

"Whatever Disneyland were paying, we'll double it for your exclusive story," said someone else.

Things were getting far too complicated. It was definitely time to be feline again. "Miaow," he said.

"I beg your pardon?"

"Purr."

"What was that?"

"Brrrrp."

"Could you speak up, please, the microphone's not picking you up."

"Purr-wurr."

The film crew and reporters had to give up. They would never get the full story. At least they had some good pictures.

Daphne got her dearest wish when her photograph appeared on Page Three of a leading national newspaper, captioned simply 'Glamour Puss'. All the other newspapers carried the story on the front page with headlines ranging from 'Cat in QE2 Mystery Plunge' to 'Saved by a Whisker'.

But the biggest surprise of all came on the TV news on the night of the event when the irrepressible Mr Sqynt appeared, confident and smiling. "Yes, Marmie," he told the interviewer. "I know him well. Good friend of mine. I've no idea how he got on the ship, not the slightest. He must have been having a quiet catnap in the back of a lorry somewhere and got carried away, by mistake like."

138

"What about this rumour that he was to be sold for millions to Disneyland?" asked the reporter.

"I don't know nothing about that," said Mr Sqynt. "But I'll say this, he's a tough little animal with a brilliant future. We're in the travel business together, you know. Purrfect colleages, purrfect, get it, eh, eh?" And he dug the reporter in the ribs."

"Ouch," said the reporter.

You'll scarcely believe it, but on the strength of his daily reports on the Catspots holiday, Mr Sqynt had secured himself a job with Jolly Hols, Unusual Travel's greatest rival. As soon as he had heard rumours of Marmaduke's escape he had been on the phone to them offering his services. At least it was one in the eye for K.G.B., he thought. It was disappointing, mind, to see yet another of his get-rich-quick schemes come to nothing. He *had* hoped that Operation Marmaduke really would make him a millionaire. 'But there's always a next time,' he said to himself. 'Eh, Arch, eh?'

MARMADUKE was relieved it was all over and he was going home. Joe was going to take him, his family and Daphne back to Chester in the coach while Mr Charabanc arranged transport for the others.

"Goodbye, Rebecca," he said with a purr. "Good luck with your singing. Goodbye, Robert, Bill, Angus. Goodbye Dan, goodbye Ben. Goodbye Mr and Mrs Friendly. And thank you *all* for everything."

"Will there be more Catspots holidays?" asked Rebecca.

"Perhaps," said Marmaduke; "we'll see."

"Goodbye Marmaduke," they all called.

"Purr, goodbye, purr."

As they sped northwards up the motorway Mr Roberts gave his family some good news.

"A cheque for £100 arrived for you, Marmaduke, just before we left home. It's your reward for capturing that vicious python Sinuous Singh. And you've had lots of cheques from Mr Charabanc."

"Oh purr. Put them all in your account and use them for the family. Purr."

"It's very good of you."

"Purr."

"Better still, I've got a job. It's on the Isle of Anglesey, Ynys Môn. So we'll be going home to our own island *and* back to Wales, the land of our fathers."

"*Yr hen wlad fy nghaddau,*" purred Marmaduke. "*Llongyfarchiadau*! Congratulations!"

"And Daphne's family have decided to move too, so you won't be losing your friend."

"Purr, wurr, wurr." Gradually the human world was receding. He stretched himself out on the upholstered seat, digging his claws satisfyingly into the soft material. "I'm a little weary," he said with a big yawn. "If you don't mind, I'll go back to being a real cat. Purr, wurr, wurr . . ."

And that was his last word.